The Plagues of Pharaoh

David Shaw

BookLocker
Trenton, Georgia

Print ISBN: 978-1-64719-554-0
Epub ISBN: 978-1-64719-555-7
Mobi ISBN: 978-1-64719-556-4

Published by BookLocker.com, Inc., Trenton, Georgia.

Printed on acid-free paper.

The characters and events in this book are fictitious. Any similarity to real persons, living or dead, is coincidental and not intended by the author.

BookLocker.com, Inc.
2022

First Edition

Library of Congress Cataloguing in Publication Data
Shaw, David
The Plagues of Pharaoh by David Shaw
Library of Congress Control Number: 2021936566

Dedication

Dedicated with thanks to my wife Elizabeth for her love and patience, my daughter Kate for her love and assistance, my daughter Olivia for her love and humor and Mike Cordera for spending so much time in my life.

Table of Contents

Chapter One - Moses

Moses knew this was a mistake. He stood in the dark anteroom of the palace, shaking his head. His trembling fingers pushed the staff of God toward his brother, Aaron.

"You should do this."

Aaron shook his head. "Remember," he said, pushing the staff back, "first, get their attention." He raised his own staff. "Rap three times. Only when they look at you do you speak. I will be right next to you."

"It is a mistake, God made a mistake, I am not right for this."

Aaron stood watching him. Moses took a deep breath, licked his lips but did not move. Aaron lay his staff against a wall and put his hands on each side of his brother's face.

"It is no mistake. *You* shall lead us, no one else." He nodded toward the door. "The time is now, go."

Moses nodded and strode into the hall that was bright with sunlight and thick with talk. Ministers of Pharaoh gesticulated and argued in soft or brittle tones. Aaron nodded, raised his staff. Moses spoke.

"You must let my people go!"

He squinted up at Pharaoh, took another breath, looked at the faces turning to him and slouched on the staff. Closing his eyes, he continued.

"To worship our God in d-d-distant lands for three days."

Silence. Moses rapped his staff on the floor. His brother Aaron spoke quietly and Moses rapped again twice. Another word from Aaron and Moses straightened and spoke forcefully.

"You must let my people go to worship our God in distant lands for three days."

Pharaoh rose, all except Moses and Aaron bowed. The throne was at the top of a ramp that ran the length of the hall to the height of two men. Sunlight poured through skylights on the god-king's practiced walk, his chin augmented by a braided gold beard, his eyes painted wide and all seeing. A blue lotus amulet swung from a leather collar.

"We have missed you like we miss a son." He displayed no anger. "This palace, this kingdom is lacking without your heart. It has been so many years."

"It has been five years and I am not your son. I am a Hebrew." Moses closed his eyes and tightened his fists. "Y-y-y." He gripped his staff, kept his eyes closed. "You must let my people go to worship our God for three days."

"Who is this God that let's your speech revert? You had taken such control when you lived here. Why would this God of Hebrews let this happen?"

"He is my God."

"Then why," Pharaoh said softly, "does he not tame your demon? When you left this palace your words were confident and correct. Now you struggle again."

"I have been given this t-t-task; it does not matter how I say it."

"Of course, it matters, you must command attention or your words become folly."

Moses watched Pharaoh complete his descent.

"You must let my people go to worship our God in the distant lands for three days."

"I raised you as my son, loved you as my son..."

"I am not your son! You must..."

"I must do as I wish and nothing more. I am Pharaoh, god-king, descendant of the gods, touched by immortality." The assembled parted as he walked toward Moses, his guards ready to place a seat should Pharaoh decide to sit.

"You are a man like all other men and you are descended from men for there is no other God."

"So say you when you are able to say anything. Your God, should there be such a God, shows weakness in his messenger. This does little to gain respect let alone fear."

They stood looking at each other as the brother of Moses stepped forward. Moses noticed him as if out of a trance.

"You must do this," Moses said, "you shall do this! Behold!"

Aaron threw his staff to the floor between Moses and Pharaoh. The second vizier to Pharaoh, a man named

Hannu, stepped forward to shield the god-king as did the guards but Pharaoh raised his hands. At the feet of Hannu the staff shook then bent and he stepped back. Slowly the staff thickened and curled and shone moist at their feet. Small cracks in the staff became eyes and a mouth as it slid across the floor and a narrow tongue darted out as it circled. It stopped before a sem-priest in a leopard skin robe, rose and hissed.

The sem-priest, a proud, unafraid man named Hartumn, sneered, "Servants of Pharaoh, throw down your staffs!"

Staffs clattered to the floor between Pharaoh and Moses. Eyes wide, Hartumn chanted words familiar to none of the assembled. The staffs slowly moved and glistened and grew thicker and longer than that which Moses' God created. Eyes and mouths opened as they slid to surround the smaller serpent.

Moses spoke, "You must let my people go to worship our God in the distant lands for three days."

Moses' arrogance was pitiful, a poor spokesman indeed for this God of the Hebrews. His power, or his God's power, was simple magic. Hartumn laughed as did Hannu and the others. Pharaoh shook his head.

"I loved you as my son but you betray me and now you betray your people!" Pharaoh said. "Now your people will make my bricks with no straw. Let your God help them with that as he helps you with your words."

Moses was bewildered. "This should not be hard for you. What do you fear?"

"I fear nothing, certainly not you."

"Behold," said Moses quietly as he pointed to the serpents created by the magic of Hartumn. They were each being eaten by the serpent of Aaron's staff making no move to escape the smaller snake. "You shall fear me," Moses said as the snake ate all the others. When the staff straightened Aaron lifted it and walked out. Moses followed.

"Be glad I leave you with your hands," said Pharaoh, "your betrayal deserves no less than their loss."

Hannu, the second vizier to Pharaoh, watched from his seat of honor. As a young man he had entered Pharaoh's court a month before the infant Moses had been found by the god-king's oldest daughter, Bithiah. Brought into the court by his father to be block assistant to the Viceroy, Hannu watched Moses grow up in luxury. While Hannu transcribed orders to the fields and overseers, Moses raced horses and learned the ways of swords. He walked the palace in pleated robes and curled sandals while Hannu wore a plain kilt. He even tamed his speech when the physicians and magicians of the court of Ramses could do nothing. Now Hannu wore the pleated robe and curled sandals of nobility. A scented cone sat on top of his wig. Moses' hair hung flat over his worn robe and he leaned heavily on his staff as he followed Aaron into the dark anteroom and out of the palace.

As second vizier, Hannu lived in the royal quarter but his home was modest. The surrounding wall was low and the stone front was simple white, unadorned by painted scenes typical of the quarter. He designed the anteroom to be small and low so when you walked into the less modest reception room it felt large and tall. This led to the courtyard garden and a pond filled with colorful fish surrounded by lotus blossoms. From the courtyard four hallways led to the quarters.

It was dusk as Hannu walked through the anteroom to the edge of the courtyard. His family was preparing for the evening; his wife Chiome helping his son Paneb light the lanterns as his daughter Lapis played gently on her flute. As a young lady of seven, Lapis was expected to play the end of the day to the god Ra who would emerge in his ship the next morning to bring warm sunlight. Hannu stopped to listen before he stepped into the courtyard. He smiled and nodded in gratitude to Ra and the moon god Khonsu for helping her to get better; while daughters of nobles were expected to ease the descent of Ra into the underworld to prepare him for battle against Apophis, some of them were able to play more soothingly than others. Of course, Hannu smiled to himself, Ra was preparing for battle, some dissonance might be appropriate.

As he stepped into the courtyard Lapis quickly finished her last few notes and skipped to him, bowing and smiling as he touched her head gently. Then she looked up and wrapped her arms around him, digging her face into his chest before backing away, long braids swinging. Paneb approached Hannu unsmiling; a tall, serious young man of seventeen. He bowed and accepted the gentle touch of his father on his shaved head. Chiome, short and sweetly full figured as befits the wife of a vizier, stayed where she was and smiled, bowing as he approached and they gently touched noses. Hannu could smell meat, perhaps pork.

When he returned from his chambers to dine, he recounted the events of Moses' entrance into the palace. As he described Hartumn's magic duplicating the magic of Moses, Chiome and Lapis smiled and laughed with him.

"Imagine the stuttering arrogance," he said, sipping his beer, "in the presence of one touched by immortality!"

Paneb did not laugh. "If the serpent of the Hebrew ate the others, doesn't that make him stronger? Why would this make you laugh?"

"It is magic, my son, simple magic. Talking of gods is crazy, magic is the realm of men."

Paneb shook his head while the rest of his family discussed the lessons Lapis had completed. When Hannu addressed Paneb he shrugged; his silence at the table was not unusual. He attended classes at the palace and Hannu wondered if this education was making him more reticent and aloof than he might have been had he begun working at ten like most boys his age. When permitted, Paneb retreated to his quarters then climbed to the roof to watch the Nile reflect stars.

The lever on Hannu's water clock woke him before dawn. He kept quiet, careful to let Chiome sleep. When he walked into the courtyard to lay out bread and beer for Ra he was surprised to see Paneb awake; typically, Hannu had to wake him. They sat on a wood bench facing east and thanked Ra for rising, dipping bread into beer, and tossing it into the pond where red and golden fish snapped at it.

"You had trouble sleeping last night?"

"Sometimes sleep just doesn't happen, father."

"Sleep is a gift of Tutu; you can't just refuse it. To refuse a gift is not only rude but unhealthy."

"I did not refuse. If she had visited me I'd have been happy to sleep."

"What's bothering you?"

He looked to his father, sipped some beer. "I wonder about that staff, the God of the Hebrews."

Hannu stood up, shaking his head. "You worry about nonsense," he said, walking heavily to his quarters. "Get ready, we leave shortly. Worry about your lessons, I hear your arithmetic is what should concern you. Don't worry about some conjuror."

Paneb's school was attached to the palace and they typically walked together in comfortable silence. This morning Hannu walked quickly while Paneb took tentative steps as if the ground might open at his feet.

Chapter Two - Blood

Hannu stopped when he entered the anteroom. He said his morning prayer, bowed his head and entered the court. There were several seated dignitaries inside and four soldiers stood near the entrance, speaking softly. Kenna, a tall, affable general, was laughing.

"It was perfectly balanced, smooth acacia, good weight. The next time Hartumn tells me to throw my staff down I'll see if he throws his own down first."

The others laughed and nodded. Hannu never carried a staff; his position did not require such trappings. He turned to Kenna.

"Hartumn is a sem-priest," Hannu said. "He keeps us holy in the eyes of Pharaoh's ancestors. Would you truly not throw down your staff had our bridge to eternity withheld his?"

Kenna's robe slid down his shoulder as he snapped quickly to his full height. He shrugged it back up and took a breath.

"I would throw my staff no matter what our bridge to eternity did with his own, my lord."

"Then what you said was a lie?"

"It was a joke, your honor."

"A joke at the expense of divinity?"

The officers stood at attention before the second vizier. Kenna swallowed.

"I...," he hung his head. "Forgive me your honor. It was ill conceived."

"Conceive no other nonsense. You are an example to all who see you, even those of the same rank," he looked around, "who should also know better." Hannu turned and found his seat near the scribes.

Pharaoh entered from his chambers in a loin cloth and allowed himself to be dressed at the foot of the throne tower. Once his amulet was placed over his crown, he ascended the tower by a set of stairs that went around the back and sides. The day was bright but the sun was still low; Hannu watched Pharaoh's silhouette against the open skylights as he said his prayer to Ra. When he descended the ramp they followed Pharaoh out to the Nile. Moses and his brother stood at the river edge.

"What," Pharaoh spoke slowly and deliberately, "do you want?"

Muttering soundlessly then looking down, Moses nodded to himself.

"It w-w-will be blood if you do not let my people go to worship our God in the distant lands for three days."

"What will be blood?"

"The Nile."

Someone laughed and Pharaoh smiled then spoke. "I have given you my patience as I loved you like a son, but you have used it up. You will leave now."

Moses told his brother to hold his staff over the Nile. Hannu thought of Paneb as the water turned a strident crimson and fish thrashed at the surface. This was strong magic, he thought, perhaps Moses' God should not be ignored. The shore erupted with screams and footsteps retreating from the defiled river.

Hartumn walked forward and lifted a dry vessel and ordered it filled from a well. The water was drawn clear and he incanted to Heka and the vessel became filled with blood.

"Your magic is no more than mine." Hartumn looked at Moses who replied angrily.

"Speak not to me at all and of all things not of your magic. There is no comparison to The Lord My God. Keep your council lest you be struck dead."

Hartumn stared but was quiet. Pharaoh, having seen his magician perform the trick that Moses had performed, commanded the overseers to double the quota of bricks the Hebrews must make before he strode back into the palace.

Lapis' exhausted sobs filled the house as Hannu entered. He followed the sound to the bath where she sat atop a bench overlooking the sunken tub filled with blood. She sat naked next to her mother, surrounded by blood-stained towels. Her flesh was white and clean but her hair was streaked with red and she sobbed as Chiome tried to comfort her.

"It will clean off, we will make you clean again my Lapis," her mother said to her softly. Lapis wailed louder when she saw her father.

Hannu said, "I will have water brought from the purest wells in the desert to clean you."

"NO," she screamed, "*No father no, I am filth, it was blood, it turned to blood look*." She pointed to the bath. "*Now get out!*" She moved to cover herself but the towels she picked up were stained and she shrieked and coughed and fell into despair. "Get out, you cannot see me like this, get out. I am filth. I am not fit for Ra or anyone. I am damned, I shall wander the land of darkness forever." She fell back into her mother's arms.

"You are innocent. The blood of some Hebrew God means nothing to you. You are of noble blood. You are pure and you will sleep in the house of the dead in comfort."

"NO! Get Out!" Her eyes widened. "So it was that Moses, you laughed and he turned my bath into blood."

"He turned the Nile into blood."

"*He turned the Nile into blood?*"

"And we will turn it back."

But she moaned and rocked in her mother's arms. "Get out, get out, get out."

Hannu ordered two servants to take camels to the hills above Tanis and bring back clean water at once. They were to ride all night and be back by dawn. His other servants dug wells away from the river until clean water bubbled up. The Nile stank with blood and dead fish. The pain of this curse of blood was strong. Unable to bathe, the Egyptians were forced to wear the same clothes throughout the day. Accustomed to scrupulous cleanliness, they could not even change their loincloths, a discomfort that surely none of their gods would forgive.

The noise of the city had often been punctuated with far away cries that most Egyptians were accustomed to; the Hebrews were working to build greater cities to the glory of Pharaoh and if pain was one of the building materials, it was all the will of the gods. Now, as the Hebrews suffered the pain of Pharaoh's anger, forced under whips to double the brick quota, their cries were heard steadily and louder as the Egyptians waited for the river to cleanse itself. Pharaoh had so commanded, patience was needed.

The dead fish were buried outside the city and in two days the water flowing north from forested regions was clearer. Pharaoh walked out to the river on the third morning. He filled his cup to the brim before a full assembly, lifted it to his lips and drank it down. Some people walked to the shore and scooped some to examine. Hesitant, they took timid sips but soon all were drinking and some laughing. The water was good. Pharaoh had saved them.

Even Lapis was able, after cleaning herself in the fine waters of Tanis, to drink but Chiome refused to order the servants to make any stew or use the water in cooking.

"Pharaoh is touched by immortality," she told her husband, "he can eat things that would kill a mortal."

Paneb seemed to agree, eating little and drinking some beer upon awakening then going without the whole day. The palace school was closed in these days of blood so the young man stayed alone in his chamber or on the roof. At dinner Paneb tasted a dry stick of wild celery and a water lily root then announced his return to school the next morning.

"My water clock is set," he faced his father. "I will rise and walk with you in the morning."

Hannu nodded. He had demanded that the school reopen; things must seem back to normal, things must *be* back to normal.

"Can you tell me, father," Paneb continued, "does the court believe we have seen the last of Moses?"

Lapis cried out at the mention of the Hebrew and Chiome glowered at Paneb.

"Talk of no such things at this table," she said. "Is that clear? Are you trying to upset your sister?"

"No, no I am sorry."

In the morning, as they walked, Paneb asked again. Hannu stopped walking and turned to him.

"He is a Hebrew and you are an Egyptian. We are not bowed slaves; we are not beholden to a God who expects magic to help his people. We are rulers and conquerors and whether or not we see Moses again is of little consequence because we will quench his stuttering fire before it can burn us."

"Has he not already burned us?"

At dusk Lapis would not play to Ra.

Chapter Three - Frogs

The next morning when the court followed Pharaoh out to the river, Moses was there. He looked burdened, gaunt, and tired.

"Let my people go. If you refuse to let them go, He will send a plague of frogs on your whole country. The Nile will teem with frogs. They will come up into your palace and your bedroom and onto your bed."

"We have ended your river of blood." Pharaoh sounded amused. "Why think we'll not end your river of frogs as well?" Hannu found comfort in these words; surely the gods would protect their chosen Egyptians. He is Pharaoh, touched by immortality, unafraid.

"Stretch out your hands," Moses said to his brother who did so.

The air filled with silence; even the flies in the river rushes stopped. There was no echoing bray of the camels, no rustle of hooves on the roads. All speech and song was sucked into a vacuum of sound. Hannu could feel the silence, it was in his fingers as he rubbed them together and in his hair under his scented cone. His eyes grew heavy and he imagined the goddess Serket guiding his soul past the scorpions who litter the path to paradise. But he was not dead, no one was being killed, this was simply silence, deep, thick silence. Pharaoh, my Pharaoh, stop this.

Moses leaned on his staff and the quiet grew to contain all of Egypt and the desert before Pharaoh broke it as he smiled then laughed. He lifted his hands toward Moses but before he could speak there was a small, green frog in each of them. Then another on his foot, and another. Hannu reached for the handle of his sword and a frog landed on it. The deep quiet broke and the air erupted in sound and stink and frogs were everywhere.

Pharaoh called Hartumn, "What can you do?"

"With the help of Heka and the gods I can do anything."

The leopard skin cloak of the sem-priest was crowded with them, moist and slippery and clutching at his cloak and wrists and legs. He raised his hands and frogs filled each palm. They jumped to his face, grabbing at his headdress and clinging as he beseeched Heka. Hannu watched, then looked at Pharaoh who covered his face with his hands. Hartumn spit as frogs slid into his mouth as he chanted.

Hannu closed his eyes and mouth when one jumped onto his nose. He could hear Hartumn above the shocked and terrified din of the city, beckoning Heka in words commanding attention.

"Thanks to Heka!" yelled Hartumn.

Hannu opened his eyes. At the feet of Hartumn sat a large, brown frog, croaking deeply. It opened its throat and erupted into two, then each doubled then all doubled again and again. The deeper croaks mixed in the air with the softer sounds of the small green ones and the magic cheered Hannu. Soon the field was filled with the large progeny of Heka who stood still or walked slowly while the smaller green frogs hopped over and among them.

"Do you see?" Pharaoh called to Moses, "Take your magic and leave, my Hebrews will never leave Egypt."

"We are not your Hebrews; we are God's Hebrews! Behold your lands awash in frogs of the Lord and heed not magic." He looked at Hartumn. "And pity the man who would perform as God."

The silence was no more, the din of croaking was everywhere and the wail of the people did not drown them out. At Pharaoh's court Hannu and the ministers made plans for their removal, but no teams were strong or large enough to make any difference. He walked home at dusk on streets full of croaking vermin; small and green and hopping and large and brown and slow that doubled then doubled again. Hannu wished he had worn thicker sandals.

Lapis ran from the courtyard to her quarters but there was no escape. She screamed and tried to rise above the floor filled with croaking monsters green and brown. Chiome brushed them off her daughter who screamed and cried and finally exhausted herself and fell whimpering onto her bed. Chiome covered her in cloaks, but they crawled underneath, and slid and jumped on her skin.

Paneb sat motionless on the roof watching the city writhe in the midst of these creatures. He listened to the screams of people finding frogs in their food and beds as they hopped on him. They caused him no harm and, as there was no end to them, there was no point in brushing them off.

"This is cursed. We are cursed," Paneb said to his father when he came onto the roof.

"It is magic run too far, my son. Hartumn created this, he went too far to show the futility of the magic of Moses. Fear not, Pharaoh is watching over us."

"This is nothing of Hartumn's. This is the Hebrew God."

"You are a child, do not try to think as a man yet." Hannu took a breath, sat down next to his son. "You can be wise beyond your years but not always. This will end. The power of Hartumn is that of Pharaoh and his ancestors of thousands of years. You shall see, he will end this."

But the frogs multiplied and there was no sleep in the city as they were in beds and clothes and even the tightest drawer or vault. Every space became filled with moist, green frogs that fit everywhere. Feet stumbled over large, brown ones that plodded and doubled before one's eyes. In the morning Hannu watched as Pharaoh summoned Hartumn while he allowed himself to be dressed, standing atop the throne tower. Even there, at that holy place of the god-king, frogs sat on the throne and bounced at Pharaoh's feet.

Hartumn entered the court in the leopard skins of his sem-priesthood, bowed his head and approached.

"Is this your doing?" Pharaoh held out his right hand and a frog was there.

"With the aid of Heka, yes, my Pharaoh."

"Can you end it?"

"Such endings are harder than simple conjuring, my Pharaoh."

"But you are working on this."

"Yes."

"And you do not protect yourself from this plague? Why is that?"

"How could I not suffer what my Pharaoh suffers?"

Once dressed, Pharaoh descended the ramp, watching Hartumn until he stepped on one of the frogs that littered the ramp and stumbled. He caught himself as a guard behind him reached to help. Pharaoh shook off the man's hand then finished his descent slowly, stepping carefully.

"That is admirable," Pharaoh replied, "that you should make yourself suffer as much as your Pharaoh does." He walked slowly around Hartumn who pivoted to keep Pharaoh in front of him. As one touched by the gods, Pharaoh could not pass sentence in words of humans, only in actions and this action of walking around Hartumn sentenced the magician to remain in place until he was released by the same action. Hannu realized that Pharaoh did not believe Hartumn; that he believed this curse of frogs was the Hebrew God's work. Pharaoh turned to his Vizier. "Summon Moses."

Moses was not long in showing himself.

"Pray to your Lord to take these away and I will permit your people to go to offer sacrifices."

Moses asked Pharaoh when to do this and Pharaoh said go tomorrow.

The frogs perished, large and small, dying where they sat, the floors and tables and land awash in the stink of their flesh. They were piled high into mounds that would not burn but only grew more foul. As the day ended, Hartumn, not a young man, still stood where he was sentenced, tiring. The dead vermin were being swept and shoveled into carts to clear the road as Hannu walked home.

Hannu wanted to feel relieved; it was over, whether Hartumn's curse or the Hebrew God's, the frogs were dead. The land was unburdened and there was clear water and food. At his house the servants cleaned everything. Chiome walked the halls in sandals and anklets of leather, making sure no corner was missed. Lapis had her feet and ankles protected as well but Paneb remained barefoot. When the bath was scrubbed, Lapis and Chiome cleaned themselves and were able to smile. Sitting at the dressing table, Lapis colored her mother then herself with azurite and fragrance. Hannu heard them as he sat with Paneb and smiled at the laughter. Then they dined on sweet fish and herbs and Lapis played her flute.

After dinner, Hannu invited Paneb to walk with him to the river. It was a clear night and the nightmare was over. Paneb rose and they put on curved tipped sandals and walked past walls so high you could not see the houses they enclosed.

"I never wanted such a high wall around my house," Hannu said, "so uninviting. And in these days what is there to be protected from? This is not ancient Egypt; this is our modern land."

Paneb said nothing and they got to the shore and stopped and looked up.

"Look at the Imperishable Stars," Hannu said. "See how they chase Sah, forever chasing Sah, never catching the great Boatman. Don't miss this lesson of the gods, my son, as the Imperishable Stars forever circle, never setting, so does our kingdom."

"Yes, father."

In the morning Hannu was relieved to see Hartumn gone. It was Hartumn's magic that caused the plague and Hartumn had ended it. When Moses came to the river to pray to His God, Pharaoh told him to stop.

"Do not bother, Moses, it was my magician's trick gone awry but he has tamed it. The Hebrews will go nowhere."

Moses looked at Pharaoh and his court behind him, some thirty men dressed in the finery of Egypt. Hannu wondered for a moment if Moses would walk to them, bow to the Pharaoh and beg forgiveness. His robe seemed more bleached and torn every time he showed himself. Could this really be what he wanted? Loved as he had once been in the palace, he could be a prince again. Moses turned and walked away, his face twisted in disappointment.

Chapter Four – Gnats and Flies

The next morning, approaching the river with Pharaoh and the court, Hannu's stomach twisted when he saw Moses yet again in front of the bullrushes. How could this stuttering fool be so thick and stupid? What had touched him that made him insane?

Moses watched them approach then spoke quietly to Aaron who touched his staff to the ground. Dust rose from it in a billowing, heaving sheath, growing wider and thicker and falling upon itself then rising higher, as if alive. Before Hannu closed his mouth gnats were inside and in his nostrils and eyes. The hum of the swarm was joined by screams as the undulating cloud spread to engulf and explore every crevasse on every person and thing in the kingdom.

Pharaoh turned and took measured steps back into the palace. As Hannu turned away he stopped to note Moses standing calmly on the shore with his brother. They watched each other; did Moses remember him? Hannu turned away.

Walking home, he saw neighbors clawing and scratching at themselves till blood was drawn. He shepherded his family into the smallest chamber, Lapis screaming and

Chiome trying to shield her with veils and her arms while Paneb waved slowly as there was nothing to be done.

Hannu wanted the Hebrews gone. He lifted Lapis and led his family into the garden where they unclothed and got quickly into the pond. The floor was slippery and the fish darted and bumped them which brought new cries from Lapis, but it also brought relief. Outside people jumped into the Nile and Hannu heard them splashing until he lowered his head into the water.

Soon the pond was layered with drowned corpses of the pestilence. Lapis whimpered as Chiome tried to caress her. When hunger rose Hannu ran to the kitchen where his servants also whimpered and shivered and he told them to get into the Nile. Finding some celery and lotus shoots, he brought them out and his family ate as best they could, no longer attempting to avoid ingesting the insects. When they grew tired their faces fell below the surface so he got some stones and put one under each of their heads so they could rest. Hannu stayed awake to watch and make sure no one slipped under. The night was spent in chilled discomfort, dreams of earthquakes and murmuring animals abounded.

Hartumn incanted and touched his staff to the ground, ingesting the insects and feeling them in his eyes and ears, but he could not create gnats out of dust. This, he told Pharaoh, is the work of a strong God and should be heeded. Pharaoh lay in his bath as servants covered themselves with veils and potions and fanned the god-king.

Moses stood untroubled in a pocket of visibly clear air the next morning. Hannu and the court and Pharaoh saw him through the veils and fabrics that covered their eyes. The Nile was filled with people escaping the swarms. There was no moaning, exhaustion had set it; children were being held at the surface, hunger tearing at them. When Moses spoke they all turned to watch and listen.

"If you do not let my people go to give sacrifice, my Lord will send flies into Egypt as numerous as these gnats to cover all and putrefy all. But you will see that only the Egyptians will suffer this and that the Hebrews in Goshen will suffer not and that will be a sign for you to heed. Notice the gnats are no more. Soon there will be flies unless you let my people go."

It was so, the gnats were no more. It was so quiet without the steady hum of tiny wings that Hannu laughed. People rose from the river and walked tiredly to the shore, some falling asleep on the sand. It must be over, Hannu knew as he walked home, unable to believe Pharaoh would not concede.

Lapis had not left the pond. When Hannu bent to lift her from the water she screamed but he soothed her and brought her to her bed. Chiome sat at her bedside and glared at Hannu then rose and walked past him to direct the cleaning. Dead gnats crunched under her sandals.

Paneb sat on his roof looking out at the Nile. His folded arms were covered with dead gnats. He blinked a few off his eyes as he looked at Hannu, then shook his head. Hannu asked him why but Paneb did not reply. Hannu sat with him and told him this would now end, but he shook his head again. They sat in silence and watched the sun set over the city. Hannu had never lacked wisdom to sooth his son; now even simple words escaped him.

Lapis would not play to Ra, even from her bed.

Hannu rose to a sunrise full of thick dust. As he walked to the palace atop the tiny dead that littered the street, he thought of Hartumn; this was magic he could not master.

Hannu's heart rose. This must now end, the Hebrews will go, Pharaoh will end these calamities.

But Pharaoh did not let them go.

When the court of Pharaoh saw Moses at the river's edge, they stopped as one. Some of them moaned, others just sighed but Hannu was disgusted.

"What new hell do you bring us now?" Although speaking before Pharaoh spoke was not tolerated, Hannu could not stop himself. "What would you have us do now?"

"Hannu!" Pharaoh's voice was abrupt and deep and his second Vizier stepped back, dropping his eyes then turning to his lord.

"Master," Hannu grew pale and wondered at his action. To cause Pharaoh to raise his voice was a grave offense. "I beg your patience."

Pharaoh waved him off and said to Moses, "What bring you now?"

"Flies, as I said yesterday." Moses looked thinner than he had even a day earlier. His hair was filled with dust and his cloak torn in new places as if he had been fighting.

His speech varied little except to announce the new horror; flies shall be everywhere, in the houses, on the roads, everywhere. His voice was clear and he did not miss any words. His Lord, he assured the Egyptians, would deal differently with the Hebrews; no flies would swarm Goshen where they lived, only the Egyptians will be plagued by them. Moses' Lord would make that distinction.

"And," Moses finished, "it will happen tomorrow."

Hannu had been careful to conceal what he knew from those he saw as he walked slowly home. He did not want to be a portent or scare them; all was awful enough, why have them know what will happen next? Each step was as if walking uphill and his eyes fluttered until he jerked his head awake. He was still shocked that he had spoken out before his god-king. And shocked that Pharaoh did not let the Hebrews go.

His neighbor Reshet stepped from his house and approached him. "Hannu, please, is there more?"

"Flies," Hannu said, not having the will to stop himself, "there will be flies."

Reshet stopped in front of Hannu, aghast, eyes wide, feet crushing the tiny dead.

"Flies?! I cannot, we cannot take this. Hannu you must do something." Reshet knelt. "My family, my children, they cannot continue in this, we will all die. Please, you must help us, you must do something."

"You will not die," Hannu shouted. He took a deep breath and gripped Reshet by his shoulders, raising him up. "You must be strong. Go to your house and seal it and make it tight and do what you can and protect your family. Pharaoh will protect Egypt."

"You must make Pharaoh do something. Egypt is in great pain; you must talk to him."

"What can a mortal say to a god-king? Pray to your gods and ready your home for flies."

"Flies?" a woman cried out and Hannu noticed an audience watching in terror and rose to his full height to speak. But murmurs grew to cries around him and the same woman said, "Did he say flies?" Words of assent caused more shrieks that echoed. They crowded to him as if he could offer help and he was jostled before he could make his way through to his house. Chiome watched him from the garden as he entered.

"Lapis has not left her bed." She had dark eyes with thick brows painted blue with red tips. Trained to keep her lips still even when speaking in the custom of Egyptian women of nobility, she looked silent as she spoke. "Paneb sits on the roof and says nothing, doesn't move, doesn't eat. Now what will be next? You know what will come."

"Flies," he said, quietly. "We must seal the house."

He ordered the servants to seal all entries. Silks and fabrics were rolled and stuffed into doorsills and thick cooking fat was used to line the thinnest of cracks. Chiome sat watching her husband direct the household.

"Is there nothing you can do?"

Hannu shook his head.

"You have the ear of Pharaoh."

"He is touched by immortality and does not listen to mortals."

Chiome turned and walked to Lapis' quarters. Hannu walked to the roof where Paneb sat. Paneb watched him approach with narrow eyes then rose to speak.

"You cannot stop the Hebrew God with this," he said, motioning to the veils and seals. "Nothing can stop him except Pharaoh, but he won't. He will see Egypt collapse before his heart is softened."

"Pharaoh is doing this for Egypt, my son."

"Pharaoh is no man to live for this terrible quest."

"He has touched infinity. He is descended of gods and unafraid."

Paneb sat down, shaking his head. Chiome lay with Lapis for another night as Hannu did what he could to seal the house until he fell to his bed in exhaustion. Paneb sat watching the stars reflect in the river until Ra heralded a new day.

Flies were everywhere. Hannu's deep sleep was broken by the screams of Lapis and Chiome. Hannu ran to their room, clamping his mouth tight and blinking into the buzzing mass that filled his halls. There was nothing he could do in Lapis' room; she lay under her sheets moaning while Chiome covered Lapis' ears with her own hands. Chiome looked up at Hannu.

"*Why can this not be stopped?*" She didn't bother warding off the flies in her face. "*You must make him end this!*"

"I dare not approach Pharaoh!"

"You must, someone must. You must save us, save your daughter!"

Hannu grabbed a perfume spray and tried to build a shield of scent around his wife and daughter. It did nothing, the flies remained everywhere.

"This will not last. Keep her safe, I will be back."

"Save us, Hannu, you must save us!"

Her words echoed in his ears even as the flies filled them and he trotted to the palace as the city began to erupt in horror at this latest of plagues. At the palace stable, hooves cracked as the horses screamed and panicked. Hannu found the stablemaster dizzy in his attempts to calm the animals.

"Prepare a chariot immediately," he told the stablemaster as he walked toward the guard house.

"These horses cannot be prepared," the stablemaster said. "Behold, you can see them with your own eyes."

Hannu turned to face him. "*Prepare a chariot or you will lose your hands. The life of your land, your Pharaoh, is at stake!*"

He left the stable and ran to the guardhouse. Three men were already roused and had thin scarves over their faces. They looked at Hannu in fear as they were swarmed.

"One of you shall ride me to Goshen. Go to the stable and help the stablemaster."

"The horses are wild, my lord. What is in Goshen?" one of them asked.

"Go do this now and do not question me. We must ride immediately."

"Can you end this? Will this end in Goshen?" But Hannu was running to the court of Pharaoh. He heard the people of the city screaming as he approached the anteroom and walked in. Ra was beginning to fill the court with fly filled, buzzing sunlight. Pharaoh had a mask of silk over his face atop his throne tower. Hannu approached as Pharaoh allowed himself to be dressed. He fell to one knee before his god-king.

"Hannu, speak."

"I ride to Goshen now to see if the words of Moses are true."

"What has he said falsely that you doubt him?"

Hannu could think of nothing Moses had said that did not come true.

"I want to see with my own eyes. There should be no flies in Goshen, as you recall, Master. Moses said so, I want to see."

"And if it is so? If there are no flies in Goshen?"

Hannu said nothing.

"The horses sound wild," Pharaoh said, "can they be used?"

"With your words and wishes they will take us to Goshen."

"Hannu, you have fumbled in words lately. Tell me, what would my second Vizier advise his Pharaoh to do?"

As second Vizier, Hanna had noble rank but never the ear of Pharaoh. That was only for the Vizier himself, or the generals or treasurers. Hartumn, of course, being sem-priest and magician, was permitted to speak and question. For Hannu to be asked to advise was a weighted honor. Remembering the short steps of Pharaoh around Hartumn, he decided to speak plainly.

"If Goshen is free of flies, as Moses said, I would advise you to heed his words and send the Hebrews to worship their God."

"Do you not think your Pharaoh has a plan?"

Hannu dropped his forehead to the floor. "Pharaoh is my god-king, touched by immortality. It is beyond my understanding to think in such terms."

"But you would suggest we allow them to leave."

"Forgive me, Master, yes. Give them three days, let us breathe again and be gone of these abominations."

"Ride to Goshen and report back today."

Chapter Five - Goshen

Two tall stallions stood strapped to a chariot of war rather than a touring vehicle, the stablemaster having rightly assumed that speed was of the essence. Leather hobbles kept their legs still though their heads bobbed and swayed in constant motion as they groaned under the flies. One of the guards stood ready to accompany Hannu, his robe short over riding chaps. Hannu recognized him as Qen, a personal favorite of the Vizier, competent and brave.

The horses would not let the stablemaster lead them to the road and he had to affix nose clamps to each to get them to follow. They screamed but stopped bobbing their heads and were easily led. As they walked the chariot to the road, Qen stepped on and took the reins. In his many expeditions and trips of diplomacy, Hannu was accustomed to touring chariots with wide platforms, seats, handles and a gate to close behind him. Chariots of war were built to accommodate a driver and an archer and had none of those. There was only a narrow floor with a short front fence, and no seats or gate. Stepping onto the platform next to Qen he bent over to grab hold.

Qen said, "We can use a touring chariot if you wish, your honor."

"We must have speed." Hannu spoke loudly. "I am ready."

"Hold on sir, the horses will bolt as soon as they are released. It is not unusual for the archer to kneel."

Hannu knelt and held on. The stablemaster left the nose clamps on the horses as he released the hobbles on their legs. Both animals now huffed loudly and held very still as he slowly unscrewed both clamps at once, readying himself to leap out of the way as soon as they were free. Hannu became impatient, watching this man unwind the clamps in tiny increments.

"Today, fool, can you feel the flies? There is urgency!"

Qen began to say something to Hannu but the stablemaster unwound both clamps too quickly and the horses screamed. Qen held tight to the reins as one of the clamps fell to the ground and that horse reared and the other screamed and the stablemaster stumbled and yanked off the other clamp and now both reared wildly as the stablemaster dove to the side.

Fearing that the violent actions of the horses would dismember the shaft and yoke, Qen gave some head to the horses and they bolted. Flies pelted their faces as the horses accelerated up the main concourse of the palace toward the city gate. Whining wheels and grinding hooves echoed in the fly laden air and Hannu knelt, holding tightly to the fence as his arms were sprayed with silt.

It was fortunate that the road was empty, as Qen was able to lead the horses but not stop them. The animals heaved and pounded through the city and under the gate. Qen turned them to the road to Goshen as Hannu held on. Hannu thought there may be less flies out of the city, but they were everywhere and he nodded grimly; why would there be less anywhere except Goshen? The horses frothed under their veils.

"We must look at their noses to make sure they aren't hurt," Qen said loudly.

"We will stop when we get to Goshen."

"My Lord, they may be gravely injured. We'll have to walk back if we do not tend to them."

"Look at them! Would you stop them? Could you? Will you stand in front and handle them now?"

"We need to slow them down, they are running too fast; we have a long way to go. Stopping them will help."

"There will be help and water in Goshen."

Qen kept his council and the horses kept to their ragged gallop. Hannu held on, the ride much rougher than any he had experienced in larger chariots and he bounced constantly. Sweat flew off the horses in a hectic spray as the sun and flies punished them. Hannu wondered if camels, less skittish with clear eyelids to protect them from the flies, would have been a better idea. Although more stubborn they would have provided an easier ride.

Then, as if riding out of a storm, the flies were gone. The horses stopped, panting in the clear air of Goshen. The chariot jolted to a halt and Hannu gripped the low fence to keep from toppling over it. He took the veil off his face and felt the dry, still air. Qen was breathing heavily next to him, slouching in relief. Hannu's knees ached as he stiffly rose and stepped down, the earth calm beneath him. He turned to Qen who stood in the chariot.

"Take off your mask, feel the sun on your face." Hannu called to him.

Qen loosened his mask. Hannu's relief at the clear air was not mirrored by Qen who looked grim and angry.

"Did you know we would leave the flies?" He tied off the reins and stepped down.

"Yes, I expected it."

"Is this what the Hebrew said would happen?"

"Yes, this is what Moses said would happen."

"They have a very powerful God."

"So, it seems."

"Yes, it does." Qen was shaking his head. "Why would our gods let this happen? Why would Pharaoh let this happen?"

"We must have faith. Do not question the gods or this will seem like a mild punishment."

"Do not question the gods? Will they punish us for wondering why they allow the Hebrew God to punish us? Don't we deserve answers?"

"For what?"

"For my piety! For my prayers and deeds, they don't earn answers?"

"They earn you eternity."

"Eternity? In my house right now, my wife suckles my son blindfolded with flies all over her tits. Forgive me, my lord, eternity can wait. We need help now; we should let these Hebrews leave."

"Our god-king and gods have plans." Hannu looked at Qen, a short, broad man with a thick neck, smart and loyal and scared. "We are tools of Pharaoh, here to assure that the words of Moses are true. So they are, so we shall report."

Qen walked in front of the horses, the dried blood fluttering as they panted. "We must find water."

A soft shake of the reins was all the horses needed. A row of low houses lay ahead and they kept a slow pace. Qen held the reins to keep the horses from breaking into what could be a deadly gallop should they smell water. Hannu stretched first his back then his knees, the jarring ride still pumping his blood.

The houses were huts with anchoring beams piercing out of the front over low doorways and windows covered with reed mats. Thick beams ran along the front of each, connecting them to each other as if banding against an enemy with only a cubit or so between them. Shimmering pale white in the rising sun, each house had small gardens of food in front. From a small plot that showed low greens like turnips, three children rose and stared before a woman ran out and pulled them inside. Behind the huts, as Hannu expected, was a stream. They were near the Oasis of Simut.

"Do we let them drink from the stream?" Qen asked.

"There must be a well. We should find it."

They were worried that the streams may be tainted, this being land inhabited by Hebrews whose ways were strange. The horses smelled the stream and strained toward it but Qen kept them on the path. Sweat glistened on their necks and manes as they panted and followed weakly.

Finding a stone well behind a corral of goats, they unhitched the horses and led them. Having nothing to put the water into, they let the horses drink from the well bucket, the dried blood clustering on the surface. Qen pulled it away every few seconds to keep them from drinking too much too fast and to satisfy his own thirst. Hannu hesitated, noting the blood and thought again about camels. Then he drank. An angry voice sounded behind them.

"It is not enough to enslave us; must you also defile our well?"

Hannu turned to watch her stomp toward them between two of the huts. She had black hair rambling down her back, wide eyes and a green stone fastened her blue tunic. Noting this, Hannu wondered how they found time to make dye.

"Your animals drink with you," she said, "do they eat with you as well?"

"It is only water."

"Or do you eat with them at their troughs?"

Neither Hannu nor Qen were accustomed to being berated by anyone much less a Hebrew but it was Qen who narrowed his eyes.

"It is only water," Hannu repeated, incredulous.

"You say that as if there was so much of it."

An older woman looked out a window. "Talmor, come back!"

Talmor ignored her. "Now the stink of your horse is in the bucket." She walked toward them and Qen stepped in front of her, his hand on his sword.

"Stand down," Hannu said but Qen remained between them.

"You beat and enslave us and now you poison our water."

"It is the well of Pharaoh as is the ground you walk on and the house you sleep in." Hannu had little patience for this. These people were not suffering; their air was clear. "If you believe these horses have tainted your water then drink from the stream. Your God and your leader Moses will kill you all, anyway."

A grim smile cross her lips. "That may be true."

"What may be true?"

"What do you know of God?" She stepped closer.

"What do you know of me? I am second vizier to Pharaoh and you dare question me? I asked *you* a question!"

"You are Egyptian!" She took another step then another and Qen unsheathed his sword. She lowered her voice and took another step. "You are all barbarians and God punishes you!"

"Qen! Stand down!"

"And you would kill anyone," she went on, "even a woman who dares question you."

Qen sheathed his sword but remained between them in his duty to protect.

The act of speaking his rank reminded Hannu of his station. He was a diplomat, fond of and skillful with words, negotiator of treaties. Anger was unseemly and he softened his voice. "I wish only to visit Goshen and see what is here. There is no ill will in this visit."

"Visit?" She spat the word. "Visitors are invited, welcome. And you have already shown yourselves to be terrible guests. You do not visit, you intrude."

"Perhaps, but intrusion is not our aim."

"What do you come to Goshen looking for?"

"Flies." Hannu saw no reason to not be truthful.

Standing barely a foot from Qen, Talmor looked at Hannu. "So, it is true."

"What do you know of it?" Qen snapped.

"Stand down, soldier!" Hannu said. "Yes, looking at Talmor, "it is true."

"Yes, I saw it. It is terrible?"

"Yes, it is terrible." Hannu looked at her. "What did you see?"

As a young girl, Talmor had watched the death of her father. While her family mourned his death she found herself suddenly able, she believed, to see and perceive things unknown to most. It was not a gift she wished for. Flies had joined her dreams of late.

Ignoring his question, she spoke. "Then why do you not do as God commands?"

"Tend to the horses," Hannu told Qen, "and ready the chariot." Qen turned to Hannu then followed his orders. Hannu looked at Talmor. "Our gods have protected us for millennia. We are a people of great faith."

"Your great faith punishes you. The river ran blood, did it not?"

"We are not going to be fooled by magic."

"Magic? Look around you! There are no flies here. Are they numerous in your city?"

"Walk toward the city for less than half a mile, there is a wall of them. You may find it wondrous."

"We do not revel in your misery; we are not like you."

"We revel in no man's misery."

She looked at him, shaking her head in wonder and squinting as if the sun was behind him.

"Do you believe that? Do you expect me to believe that?"

"Sometimes a nation must act offensively to protect its people."

"Act offensively? My father worked on a tower built on quicksand. On quicksand! When it finally toppled, the falling stones killed dozens." Her eyes were wide with anger. "I watched my father get crushed under one of your giant stones! Is this acting offensively? Is this not causing misery for no reason? Why else would you command that then to revel in it?"

"I am sure no one knew it was on quicksand."

"Have you seen quicksand? We knew! My father knew!"

Knowing nothing of this, Hannu was stunned. "Rinse and boil your bucket, there should be no harm to it. We meant none and will be on our way."

She did not move as he walked away. Qen was able to sooth the horses enough so that he could look at their noses and rinse off what dried blood was left. The fact that he was able to touch them at all was good news.

"Those nose clamps, they are barbaric, beneath this nation."

"We are a nation of strength!" Hannu snapped. "In the service of our nation we must sometimes resort to barbarism. Like any tool, like a chariot or a whip. These things must be handled properly but they must be handled!"

They passed villages as close and tight as the first one; clean and orderly with white walls and sunny gardens suffused with quiet darkness. Apart from the occasional bleat of a lamb there were no sounds, not of commerce, of children, not even any noises from the streams and thankfully not of flies. And there were no men. The occasional child or woman they saw ran immediately away, the men seemingly working on Pharaoh's projects. As it should be, Hannu thought. If this moody silence is the price they pay, so be it; Egypt is paying a higher price now because of them.

Before mid-day they turned around and headed back. They stopped at the same well but Hannu kept Qen from letting the horses drink from the bucket. He instructed the guard to dig a hole with his sword and Hannu removed one of his veils and laid it in, then poured in water, and the veil kept the water from seeping into the sand long enough for the horses to drink. Then they filled the waterskins and left.

The horses did not take well to the chariot hitch; they stood still but moaned and whined quietly. Walking slowly up the road they heard a low murmur in the distance, building slowly. Hannu suspected an earthquake. He had heard them approach before, felt the ground shudder, saw the hesitation in the horses, their breath quickening. They tried to dart sideways and remained straight only under Qen's whip.

There was no earthquake, it was the flies that greeted them as they left Goshen and the horses stopped and reared, unwilling to go on. Hannu signaled Qen to step down and they calmed the animals as best they could. They wrapped fabric over their faces but that agitated them again and they refused to move further.

"We must lead them," Hannu said. "Let them get used to the flies and we will climb on down the road." Qen looked at Hannu doubtfully but took a bridle and tried to lead one as Hannu handled the other. They would not go into the flies. No pulling or whipping would move them.

"Perhaps we unhitch and try to ride them?"

"My Lord, the way they will run, I doubt we can hold on. We can unhitch them and try to walk them slowly without the chariot."

"Leaving it here, with the Hebrews?"

"Do we have a choice? And what can they possibly do with one chariot? Do they even have horses?"

"We should have taken camels. I do not like leaving the chariot here."

Qen began unhitching one horse and Hannu wondered if he heard him. Leaving the chariot for the Hebrews was a difficult option.

"Wait," he said, "let's try walking them around to calm them. Perhaps if we walk them close to the flies before entering they will relax."

"Yes, sir," Qen said, though obviously leery of this plan. He hitched the horse back up and each took a bridle and walked slowly along the line of flies. The horses stepped in a slow, crooked pace. "We must talk, it will calm them."

"Tell me about your family," Hannu asked.

"My family. Not much to tell. I have a young son of three months and my daughter is seven."

"And her mother? How long have you been married to her?"

"Her mother is dead as are her two younger sisters. My wife is quite sweet, if simple. I think she'll make a good mother if her children live."

"By the will of the gods they will live long and fruitfully."

"Yes, let us hope. My daughter is a strong girl and should pass into womanhood. Maat is her name."

"And your son's name?"

"My lord, he is three months old, why tempt the gods and name him? Even should he pass a year we cannot get too fond of him; I have lost two already. Now I finally have a boy, a little fat one, too, and I pray every morning he makes it through the day."

Hannu was reminded of his station in Egypt. His children had the palace physicians and services available. The average Egyptian had only some herbs or leeches should their children fall ill.

"And your wife? Tell me about her."

"Her name is Masika, born during the rain. She is around eighteen, thick and healthy."

"Pretty?"

"No."

"You said she was simple?"

"Yes," he chuckled to himself. "She is half my age; we don't have much to talk about. She is not a curious woman but she takes care of my daughter."

The horses' pace steadied as they walked and Qen steered them slightly closer to the flies.

"We must try soon, my lord."

"As you see fit."

Qen angled them slightly toward the noisy line then closer, and both men put on veils and led the horses in. Both horses shook their heads and whined but kept a calm pace until the noise and flies surrounded them. Hannu was beginning to feel confident that his idea worked even as flies tried to enter his ears through the veil. He pressed the fabric against both sides of his head and it fluttered violently.

No less harassed were the horses whose ears and eyes were under constant pressure. The older stallion was not yet healed from the nose clamp and turned and rubbed it on the other horse's flank. That brought no comfort to the poor animal, only a new trickle of blood which the flies found immediately. He snorted into the veil, blowing it up for a moment, and his nose became covered as the flies dug at the blood and fought each other for the feast.

Hannu and Qen did not know what caused the stallion to rear and try to dart. The other horse was jerked and lost his footing and both fell to the ground. Panicked, they rose quickly and broke into a trot then spun in fear as the flies thickened and the chariot swung out. Hannu jumped back and watched the chariot bounce as the horses galloped toward Goshen into clean air. He wondered that the wheels did not break as the horses jumped a low ridge of rocks. The chariot bounced over it and the draught pole broke and the bridle snapped and the horses ran hard, connected by the harness, into Goshen. The chariot tumbled to a halt and stopped among the rocks.

Hannu ran back out of the flies and watched the horses thunder into the distance. They faded quickly from sight then seemed to slow down, but he could not tell, so far had they run. He was moist with sweat but the air was clear. Looking for Qen in the fly-soaked haze, he saw nothing. Inhaling deeply, he stepped toward the wall and looked closely. There was a pile of rags and riding mail shimmering, unmoving, on the sand.

Running into the buzzing mist he gripped Qen's arms and pulled him into the clear air. There was blood on his face and one of his legs turned outside at the knee. Hannu tried to find someplace soft to lay him, dragging him further back from the flies until he sank in exhaustion and let Qen lay where he was. Splayed face down on the warm sand, he dug his knees in and turned his face to the earth, closed his eyes and thought again about camels.

Qen did not move. Hannu saw no breathing. Dare he ask for help from the Hebrews? Would they even consider helping or would they just kill him, or both of them? He was sure that he could not leave him. Opening his robe, Hannu spread it over Qen and walked to the chariot.

It seemed undamaged, the front frame intact, the pole broken a cubit from the fence. The rest of the pole rode deep into Goshen now between the two horses. He lifted the broken end of the pole and the chariot rose with him. Imagining no other way to transport Qen, he pulled the vehicle off the rocks and onto the sand into which the thin wheels sank. Grunting, he dug in, and Hannu swore to his own gods and others and found the strength to pull it next to Qen.

There was a skin of water in the side basket and he pulled it out and took a small sip. Kneeling he dripped some into Qen's mouth to no result. If the man is dead, he thought, what is the point of bringing him back? Would the

Hebrews defile his remains? And if he is not dead? He knelt now and gripped the man under his arms then stood up. Panting heavily, he lifted Qen and laid him curled on the floor of the chariot, then replaced his robe over him before falling back to the sand. He must get help. Or pull him to the city. There was a road; he knew that the horses, as difficult as they were, had used it for most of their journey. He would not be able to pull Qen on the sand, he must find the road.

Rising he slowly walked parallel to the noisy wall of flies, kicking into the sand at intervals to find the firmer footing of the road. After pacing out perhaps a mile he reversed and began the other direction, stumbling in the heat. How would he possibly do this? If he even found the road the walk would be unbearable amid the flies and sun. Despair set in as he realized he would have to leave Qen behind to save his own life. Or he must ask the Hebrews for help. Then his foot hit firm ground, barely hidden by the blowing sands. He dropped to his knees and brushed clean this patch of the packed road that the Hebrew slaves used for decades to come to work in the city. Surely this was a sign, here in the realm of Ra, that he must bring back the fallen soldier.

As he trudged back along the road to the chariot he prayed for strength and forgiveness. He was not an evil man, but not humble either, and the gods treasured humility. Having sworn and cursed them earlier he understood that finding the road meant he had a duty to fulfill to obtain forgiveness, and he was heartened by this simplicity.

The chariot was less than a dozen cubits from the road and its balance made it easy to lift. Pulling it through the sand to the road with Qen was difficult, but when he got to the road it was so much easier that his spirits rose.

Placing a cone on his head then a short robe over it afforded some meager shade. Hannu gripped the draught pole and plunged into the living wall, his ears filling with the cacophony of wings. Putting his head down, he ground his legs into the road to gain some slight momentum, but no steps were easier than others. Bent under the sun which, in ordinary times, would send these insects to cover, he walked on. Ra was becoming fierce and Hannu, a man trained for consulting with ministers in the palace and not desert expeditions, faltered. He took a tiny sip from his waterbag but dared not stop walking; the flies doubled if he hesitated.

Hannu's ears felt on fire but when he put a hand over one, flies got trapped against the veil and grew agitated and louder. He closed his eyes for minutes at a time, feeling the road and hoping Ra would steer him straight. When his back ached, he turned around and tied the remains of the leather bridle around his waist, flexed his thighs and leaned, walking backwards, toward the city. Goshen faded too slowly from his sight behind the chariot.

Qen had not asked him about his family so Hannu decided to enlighten him.

"My wife," his voice cracked so he took another short sip of water and spoke quietly, "she is thick like yours but far from simple. Sometimes I wish she was."

He watched the soldier for any movement, then yawned and quickly clamped his lips against the flies who tried to dart past the veil and into his mouth. Flies were all over the robe over Qen, head to toe, and Hannu blew at them out of habit, breaths that did not pass his veil. He looked at the horizon and wondered how long they had been moving.

"My daughter is Lapis, a child, just seven. She is smart and her mother teaches her letters and music and she plays her flute to bid farewell to Ra every evening. Most evenings I am sure Ra is eager to flee her playing."

There was water, shimmering in the desert in Goshen not too far off, a wide expanse. How had he missed it? He stopped and looked as it rippled in the sun. It was far off, had he turned? Ra continued his rebirth in the same part of the sky and Hannu was still on the road. How could that be there? He set the chariot down and took a few puzzled steps toward what seemed a low lake. It would not help. Going back would only lengthen the trip. He had water and what strength he had must bring them to the city. He had none to spare.

He turned slowly, watching the horizon in all directions. The lake spread as he watched, shining silver, surrounding him. Facing the city, he watched it cross the road in front of him and knew it was a mirage, nothing to go to, nothing to avoid or aim for, nothing. Not even a dream or an ill-fated idea, just nonsense, a trick of Ra or of some god. Was it the Hebrew God, that vengeful torturer, luring him into exhaustion? Did that God find Hannu arrogant for this excursion? Was there any meaning at all? He wrapped the strap back around him, faced Qen, dug in his heels and his thighs flexed and drove them on. What if there was nothing, no meaning, just dangerous illusions?

"My son is Paneb," he continued to Qen, "seventeen and too wise for his age. Such melancholy should only grip adults, and I worry for the boy, but he is smart and will do well."

The false lake behind them grew wider but no more distant. Paneb had called Pharaoh a man. He is no man to live for this terrible quest is what his son said. Hannu was shocked to hear his son say this but he kept it to himself; it would only have heightened the boy's melancholy. But even Chiome spoke as if the god-king is less than touched by immortality, as if Hannu could convince him that the plans of gods may have fault.

He watched his tracks behind them in the thin sand atop the road and slipped into an easy cadence, sand sliding among the flies between his feet and sandals, crushed and dry. Closing his eyes, he dreamed of dried herbs stuffed bitter into his mouth and he sucked and tore at them. Waking to flies he turned and faced the city and pulled.

One leg led the other. He adjusted the leather so it was at his shoulders and he could lean forward into his steps. His eyes closed and Lapis was bidding Ra a safe trip on her flute, jagged and dissonant. Chiome sang in a language he did not recognize and Paneb's voice joined. Then it faded into the sweet trickle of a clarinet that lifted his heart and grew louder, joined in voice by dozens, then hundreds with strange words he did not know. If the sky would have taken him he would have gone; instead, the earth found him and he was grateful and took another step, and another.

More steps followed before he turned around and leaned backwards and took more, keeping Ra at the right place in the sky and the road under his feet. His career had been full and worthy and he took note of the peace that had blessed the nation while he helped govern, his own words salving enemy wounds which would have emboldened a lesser man to violence. A man of peace, he wished only for his nation to cause no wars and make diplomacy their defense.

The Hebrews would not be availed of his diplomacy; this was Pharaoh's matter. His god-king was ruling this calamity from heaven, touched, as he is, by immortality. He must not fail. His gods were peaceful and knowing as were the Egyptians. The Hebrew he met earlier was strident but did not seem cruel; was it as well with her God?

"She is not simple," he said softly to Qen. "With Talmor you would have much to talk about. You want curious, my friend?" He smiled. "A difficult woman." What did she know of Moses? What did she see, flies? He turned around and faced the city and plunged on. Closing his eyes, he leaned against the straps and tried to imagine those dark eyes softening to him, that long hair lacing over his face.

Then he was on his knees leaning forward against the chariot strap and the gods were calling him.

"Hannu! My lord Hannu!"

There was nothing before him but flies and he closed his eyes to reenter his dream and join the comfort of the gods. When they trickled cool sweetness over his face, he fell again into that world and listened to tuneful, strange tongues. He did not feel it as he was lifted onto a touring chariot. He woke in a shallow pool of the palace garden, his head braced on the lap of a handmaiden of Pharaoh.

The sun was faltering, the flies remained. She was pouring water over him which eased the touch of the flies but not their sounds. She told a guard to get the Vizier, but it was Pharaoh who strode into the garden. Hannu tried to rise from the water. He was naked and fell to his knees.

"You may lay down before your Pharaoh."

The handmaiden put hands on his shoulders and pulled him gently back and continued to rinse him.

"Can you report?" Pharaoh stood at the edge of the pool. Hannu's eyes closed and he slid into a dream where none of the words were strange. When water was dripped onto his face he smiled. Pharaoh found that amusing and spoke softly. "Hannu, your god-king stands before you, can you wake and report?"

Report. Hannu woke and again tried to stand. Was he in the palace? The sky was beginning to darken. If this were part of his final voyage there would be no flies. How long had he been here? Where was Qen? Pharaoh sat on a bench. Hannu raised his head.

"Lay down, you need to rest."

"Am I dead?"

"You are not. Your guard is."

"No, he is not, I pulled him from Goshen."

"Yes, a dead man, you pulled a dead man in a chariot. My guards found you less than a mile from the city gate."

"Dead? No, he cannot be."

"Do you trust your Pharaoh?"

"Can you bring him back?" Hannu sat up. "Please, I trust my Pharaoh, bring him back. He has a young wife, children, he must not be dead."

"Qen is dead and I do not use my powers to revive those that have earned their rest as he has."

"But his wife, his son..."

"Hannu." As a god-king one heard Pharaoh's voice even in a whisper. He raised it now and Hannu felt the handmaiden shudder. "I need you to report."

"Forgive me, what was I reporting?" His head was spinning.

"Is the air in Goshen cursed with flies?"

Goshen, a cursed place, nasty Hebrews complaining about nothing.

"Hannu." Pharaoh rose and bent at the edge of the pool. "Your guard is dead. You brought him back, we will mourn him properly; I am having him prepared."

"He was a good man. The horses would not go back into the flies, master, I had to pull him."

"So, when you arrived at Goshen there were no flies?"

"It was like riding out of a storm, master, but the horses would not ride back." His eyes filled. Qen was dead. "I am sorry, they reared and ran and now he is dead." Who were these tears for? He hardly knew the man, brought him back, at least he tried to bring him back. "The horses, they are gone, I am sorry. They ran from the flies." He closed his eyes again, sobbing. The handmaiden poured water over his face. Opening his eyes he saw his god-king watching him. Shocked at his actions he sat up then rose to full height, naked before his god-king.

"It is as Moses said, master, they walk in comfort in Goshen. There are no flies. Forgive me, my lord."

"You are forgiven for nothing as there is nothing to forgive. You risked your life to bring back a good man."

"There are no flies."

"Yes, as we suspected. We must talk with Moses now," Pharaoh said, "at once."

Chapter Six – Livestock

Pharaoh sat atop his throne in a gold robe and a collar of bone and shells. He had no veil over his face and did not worry at the flies. Atop his wig he wore a scented cone, on his chin was a beard of braided silver. It was dusk when Hannu, dressed in laundered robes, entered the court, bowed, and took his seat. Soon Moses walked out of the anteroom, glancing around nervously, his brother behind him. Flies did not swarm Moses or his brother, the clear air around them visible in the growing darkness. What more could Pharaoh need to see?

The room was darkening, no torches had yet been lit.

Pharaoh spoke. "I understand that your people must make your sacrifices but you must do so in this land."

Moses searched the room until his eyes found Pharaoh atop his throne tower. He looked up, swallowed, shook his head.

"The sacrifices we offer the Lord our God would be d-d-detestable to the Egyptians," Moses said. He took a deep breath, closed his eyes. "And if we offer sacrifices that are detestable in their eyes, will they n-n-not stone us? My people must journey three days into the wilderness."

"I will place guards so that no Egyptian will witness your sacrifice. You shall do so in my land."

"My people must journey three days into the wilderness."

Through the haze of flies Hannu could see Pharaoh close his eyes.

"Very well. Very well but you shall not take them too far and you must end this plague and you must pray for me to your God."

"There is no other God to pray to!"

"Then do so immediately."

"I shall but do not be deceitful or it will end badly."

"Do not appear to know my ways or thoughts."

"God knows your ways and thoughts."

Moses turned and left and shortly there was not a living fly in the city. Hannu walked home in quiet darkness. Chiome was helping the servants sweep the rooms, there was much to be done, much to be laundered. Lapis was in her chambers and rose from her bed as he walked in.

"Are they gone, father? The flies, the Hebrews, are they all gone? Paneb says this will only end when the Hebrews are gone."

"They will be gone soon, my dove, and we shall live in peace again."

"Are you sure? Paneb says Pharaoh will not let them leave."

"Paneb is a child not much older than you. Don't worry, Pharaoh is taking care of us." He sat on her bed and touched her arm softly. "Come dress and let's clean the garden and enjoy the clear air."

He found Paneb on the roof.

"Help us clean the garden so we can enjoy the evening together."

"There will be worse tomorrow, why clean what will be the least of our fears?"

"The Hebrews will leave, Pharaoh gave permission, they will not go far."

Paneb looked at his father and said nothing. Then, something decided, he stood up and smiled.

"Yes, let us enjoy an evening together."

In the morning Moses was at the Nile. "You have again dealt in deceit." His voice rang strong but he looked worn, sad.

Hannu looked at Pharaoh, had he not granted permission for the Hebrews to leave? Pharaoh turned from Moses and looked at his ministers.

"I have touched immortality." His voice was soft but firm. "Am I not descended of gods?"

They watched the god-king as his eyes roamed theirs as if searching for an answer but there could only be one answer; Pharaoh was of the gods and always right. He turned to Moses and his voice was loud and firm.

"I am descended of gods and unafraid and your people will serve at my favor forever." The words sought to declare majesty but his eyes did not shine.

Then Moses spoke as loud. "Hear me, deceitful being. You will let my people go to worship our Lord the true God or you shall suffer a wrath unimagined. A new plague, a plague on your livestock, on your donkeys and cattle and sheep, all of them will perish in this new plague and the Lord our God will withhold this plague from the people of Israel. This you must do."

They looked at Pharaoh as he rose to his height, smiled without humor and said nothing.

"Pharaoh, you must do this." Moses stepped toward him and the guards stepped in front of him. "Please, I would beg on my knees but it would incite the wrath of my Lord. You must do this; you are condemning Egypt to a sad end. Let me take them and stop this."

"I stop what I want to stop."

"Is this what you want?" Moses cried, waving his hands. "The frogs, the gnats, the pestilence, this you wanted, this you created?"

"Do not try to understand the workings of the divine, Moses, leave my presence."

"Tomorrow you shall see what your presence creates."

Pharaoh spun so fast and his guards followed so close that none of his court were able to counsel with him. Hannu had seen the flies ignore Goshen and the Hebrews. This new pestilence, he was sure, would do the same. He wanted to tell Pharaoh, he was not an unreasonable man and certainly not a stupid one. What was his plan, this divine being touched by immortality? But Hannu stayed by the Nile watching Moses walk with his brother, staff in hand, into the bullrushes. He decided not to meet with any of the court this day.

As he walked quickly home the people were stirring with good humor. If the flies were gone, it was reasoned, the nightmare was over. Hannu walked quickly and smiled when someone caught his eye but he kept to himself, not wanting to hinder the unfounded optimism. He did not understand why his Pharaoh was sentencing Egypt to starvation as he was sure all of the livestock would die in the morning. He walked past piles of flies swept into unshaded places to be desiccated by Ra. Would they all end up desiccated and dried out as Qen would have had Hannu not brought him back? Might this be the fate of Egypt at the hands of Moses and this God of the Hebrews?

To his delight he was greeted by Lapis.

"Mother said it's over, father, it is time to be happy and I will play to Ra tonight to help him on his journey." She was her old bounding self, hopping from foot to foot then walking atop the low wall around the house. "Come let us enjoy, I will bring lunch to you after I feed Meres, sit in the garden and don't move!"

She ran out to tend to her lamb, Meresankh. Would the God of the Hebrews spare the lambs? Why would He, what compassion has He shown so far? And why would Chiome tell Lapis all was well? Seeing his daughter as she had been only a few weeks ago was sweet to his eyes but he must tell Chiome not to lift the hopes of anyone especially their children. There was darkness in the future.

He found Chiome tasking the servants with a special dinner.

"My love, the air is so quiet and still and the monsters are gone. We can celebrate, we *shall* celebrate!" She directed that a clutch of hedgehogs be baked in clay while a swan had been slaughtered that morning and was hung already. It would be roasted with garlic and papyrus stalks.

"I see," Hannu said, "but what did you tell Lapis."

She stopped then walked up to him and pulled him close.

"I told her it was over, all of it, I could not stand to see her like that anymore. And do not tell me if it is not true, I do not want to know."

"If it is not she will be broken with sorrow."

"She is broken with sorrow already!" She kept her voice low and walked him away from the kitchen. "We have our daughter back, at least for now and until... until forever! Look at her, she's going to feed you lunch and dinner, she is so happy. Hannu, please, I cannot watch her be so unhappy anymore, I cannot." She leaned toward him and wept softly into his chest. "You were confident Pharaoh would give in, were you not?"

"A glorious feast! Hedgehogs, how wonderful, and I'll have spines to pick my teeth as we eat." He laughed but she did not.

"What comes next, Hannu?"

He shook his head as if he didn't know. As he walked to meet Lapis in the garden, Chiome stood watching him walk away. That evening Hannu walked to the roof to bring Paneb down for dinner. His son was slow getting up.

"Lapis said it's over. She said that mother said it's over."

"So she said, yes, now let's feast the rising dusk."

"It is not over."

"How do you know this, Paneb?" Hannu had trouble keeping the irritation out of his voice. "My son, what makes you think the nightmare is not over? Look, there are no flies anymore, nor gnats."

"Our Pharaoh is a weak man; he cannot fight the will of this Hebrew God who wants us dead."

"Paneb, how can you speak such things? You must mind and be careful, such words can be dangerous, the gods hear all."

"They do not hear our cries..."

"They hear all!" Hannu took a deep breath. "Come, let us feast."

"I am sorry, my father, I do not know how I know this, it is not knowledge I wish to have."

"I know, I know, come, let us enjoy."

Camels awoke braying and their heads towered over the streets of the city, but no sheep or cow made a sound. The quaint grunt of pigs did not disturb the slow dawn. Meresankh, Lapis' lamb, lay dead in her pen. Hannu thought of staying home, Lapis would be beside herself and Chiome would pay a price for lying to her. But Pharaoh must be told, he must settle this and save them.

He walked in silence that echoed among the city to the palace until the silence broke slowly as the people rose and saw and screamed this must end, this must end, why do we not let them go? They came to the palace and stood as one as Pharaoh came out and walked to the Nile and raised his arms for silence.

"My people listen to me. Do not pretend to understand the divine plan of your ruler who is touched by immortality! You are in my care always, fear not."

None dared speak but instead fell back to begin the work of tending to the carcasses of livestock. Pharaoh sent guards to see what was happening in Goshen. Hannu was sure that, as with the flies, this plague touched not the

Hebrews. As Pharaoh watched the guards trot to the stable Hannu began to approach him.

Hartumn reached out a hand and stopped him, keeping his voice soft. "He must have all his power to fight this magic, do not distract him."

"You well know this is not magic. This is a cruel God who will destroy Egypt."

"It is cruel magic. I have studied on this! Do not forget I am sem-priest!"

Hannu spoke loud enough for his god-king to hear. "Will my Pharaoh take no council?"

Pharaoh turned his head slowly to Hannu. "I take council from my father and his father and the fathers of Ra and Amon." Then he spun and walked into the palace, closing himself in his chambers where only Hartumn could follow.

At home Hannu saw Lapis lay in the garden over Meresankh, her dead lamb, which was wrapped in a shroud of lettuce leaves. Paneb sat silently in his chambers. Chiome was still in bed. The house was quiet except the whimpering of Lapis. When Hannu touched Chiome she rolled over and covered her head and hair.

"I know, I should have said nothing but I beg you, I needed to see my Lapis again. And Paneb, he almost was smiling last night, did you see?"

"Yes, yes, I saw, it was a wonderful night."

He lay next to her. Soon Lapis appeared and slid crying between her parents. Hannu, who rose to great heights as the man who could argue and convince even the most hardheaded of enemies, was silent and had no words for his daughter that would not be lies.

Chapter Seven – Boils, Hail, Locusts

Hunger was a new fear for Egyptians. It crept into their thoughts as some butchered the dead livestock and others even attempted to cook and eat the foul meat. The smoke of those fires burned green and stank. Some retched, others could only spit and all avoided the smoke and rushed to bury the tainted flesh. They checked their fields for the health of the barley and spelt and worried over the wheat and flax. Reassuring as the crops were, the loss of meat fed their anxiety. That rats and fowl remained plentiful was reassuring but the Nile gave up few fish since the plague of blood and those were small and immature.

This plague did not touch the Hebrews. Guards returned from Goshen with a few dead sheep and goats that were captured live then succumbed as they were carried into the city. When they slaughtered a lamb in Goshen and roasted it the meat turned bad just as the guards brought it to their mouths to eat; the stench making them throw it into the fire and watched maggots writhe. This God of the Hebrews proved not only cruel but wily as well.

Fences were built and dug deep to hold hedgehogs which many now worked to trap. Rats were added to these pens but flattened themselves out and escaped. Fear of hunger panicked many, others cried, checking then rechecking the meager stores they had put aside. This was the great nation of Egypt, civilized and modern, how were they reduced to such terror?

For three days Pharaoh went unseen as the people wondered what would happen and what kinds of food supplies were set aside and when might they be allowed to partake. Hannu and the Vizier were well aware of what had been saved. It was late in a lean year though the upcoming harvest looked good. Stored grain was not plentiful; there was enough to hold off disaster for three months. People were told to pray to Renenet to provide snakes and to their own gods to protect the crops.

Moses crouched alone at the Nile before a smoldering fire of dried bullrushes. That he was not standing gave Hannu hope; perhaps this was a sign. As Pharaoh and the court walked out Moses rose from before the fire, reached down and brought his hand up black with ashes.

"You still refuse to let my people go; this is in your heart. You will now suffer boils, behold the puss ridden flesh of Egypt!"

Moses tossed the handful of ashes into the air. The cry that erupted next to Hannu was Hartumn who ran before Pharaoh, his face aflame with hideous growths, and fell to his knees. Thick yellow pus then dripped from Pharaoh's face as Hannu felt his skin tighten and pop. Hannu watched as fear grew in Pharaoh's eyes as his skin rumbled with boils. Could he be scared? Touched by immortality, what could he fear and how could this mortal disease scar the face of the god-king? Pharaoh lifted his shoulders and arms as they dripped stench and walked into the palace.

The people sobbed quietly as Hannu walked home. Lapis moaned with veils over her face and Chiome lay in bed. When he entered his son's chambers Paneb stood and walked to the window and looked at the palace, blinking as puss ran over his eyes.

"This God of the Hebrews, father, this God shall kill me."

How does a man listen to his son predict his death? How evil must this God, must these Hebrews be, to cause a man to hear his son prophesize such things? To lose a child, how does one prepare? Was there any possible logic; any words or prayers one could say?

"I will not let that happen."

"Thank you, my father, there is nothing to be done, this cannot be prevented even by Pharaoh. It is gone too far."

"My son..."

"No, don't fear this and don't mourn this, I go with ease but not yet, we have days together still."

In the morning stood Moses with Aaron before Pharaoh. "God could have slain you and all of your people but He did not. He could have stretched out His hand and struck you and your people with a plague that would have wiped you off the earth. But He has raised you up for this very purpose, that He might show you His power and that His name might be proclaimed in all the earth. Still, you set yourself against my people and will not let them go."

Pharaoh watched and listened and there was hope in Hannu's heart.

"I tell you now Pharaoh, what you have left, the animals and people in the field or outside, you must bring these into shelter for I shall raise my hands to the sky and hail will fall on every person and animal that has not been brought in and they will die."

Hannu ordered a guard to run to his home and have his servants bring the animals and servants inside. A few other of the court did as well and the Vizier ordered criers to run the streets and warn people. But Pharaoh and a few ministers stood watching, unable or unwilling to believe, even after all that had happened, even as the boils on their faces were barely healed, that this Hebrew could bring such a storm.

When there was time enough for those who would to reach safety, Moses raised his staff and lightning crashed to the ground in a bolt as long as the sky. Thunder echoed the fierce light then hail blasted the earth raising a shattering din that struck all of Egypt. Everything in the fields—people, plants and animals, were crushed and slaughtered. Every leaf was shredded, every tree stripped. The only place it did not hail was Goshen.

There was hail and fire flashing continually in the midst of it, so heavy as had never been in all the land of Egypt since it became a nation. Thunder drowned every sound as hot lighting flashed horizon to horizon. In the fields the flax which was in bloom and barley which was barely headed were destroyed. Mercifully, the wheat and spelt were not destroyed, because they ripen later and those that considered this had hope that a famine could be avoided. Most only assumed destruction was near and mourned.

Pharaoh called Moses and Aaron to his court where the clatter of hail echoed through the skylights. He waited on the floor for them to come through the anteroom.

"This time I have sinned," Pharaoh yelled to Moses over the din of the storm, "you and your God are right, I and my people are wrong. Pray for this to end and you shall go and do not stay any longer."

"When I am out of the city I will pray and beg God to stop so you may finally know but you still trust and fear not the Lord and will betray yet again."

Hannu knew that what Moses said was true. He followed Moses and Aaron to the main palace door but could not follow them outside. He was able to see the clear air protecting them amid the explosive storm as they walked in haste toward the city gate. After a few minutes the storm stopped.

Pharaoh took note and climbed the steps to his throne. Sitting heavily, he looked down at his courtiers.

"Do you see this? Do you see the power of your Pharaoh? Of your gods? Behold the silence."

Pharaoh ordered the guards to stop the Hebrews. Tomorrow would be another calamity, Hannu knew, and he walked home slowly through puddles of melted hail.

Two dead servants lay on the road, their faces and heads ground and crushed. At his house one of Chiome's cats lay in pummeled death at the front door. Bowing to this most ominous death, he lifted the dead animal and lay it at the low wall of the house where the sun would warm it and allow it to Join Ra. He went inside to the garden, the center of his family. Kneeling in the shallow pool, now adrift with broken lilies and dead fish, Hannu wept. His son, he now knew his son was going to die and he was powerless. Could there have been a moment when he could have changed this? Lapis, was she, too, doomed? Were they all? Hannu had no words to sway Pharaoh who took the council of the gods if they would only speak.

In the morning Hannu walked through a crowd to the palace, people waiting to see what the Hebrew was next going to burden them with. Moses was at the river, standing tall and even his faded robe seemed less threadbare. He did not stutter before this crowd but spoke out clearly.

"You must not refuse to humble yourself to God. Let my people go so we may worship Him or He will bring locusts into your country. They will cover the face of the ground so that it cannot be seen. They will devour what little you have left after the hail, including every tree that is growing in your fields. They will fill your houses and those of all your officials and all Egyptians—something neither your parents nor your ancestors have ever seen from the day they settled in this land until now."

The people cried and begged Pharaoh, release these Hebrews before all is lost.

"How long," some yelled to the shock of the court and the crowd, "will this man snare us? Egypt is ruined but we still have our lives."

Pharaoh heard the cries and said to Moses, "Go and worship your God but tell me who is going."

"We will go with our young and our old, with our sons and our daughters, and with our flocks and herds, because we are to celebrate a festival to the Lord."

"Your Lord be with you if I let you bring your women and children," sneered Pharaoh and the crowd moaned as Hannu's heart sank. "Clearly you are bent on evil. No! Have only the men go and worship your Lord since that's what you have been asking for. Now leave me and go perform your worship."

As Hannu walked home a wind grew from the East such as no Egyptian had known. It sliced and danced and surrounded everything. At his home all was broken and sad as he closed all doors and shutters and sealed all crevices as night fell.

The wind did not stop, it slammed what could be beaten and the walls of the house cried and the Nile blasted the shore. In the morning the wind became locusts. They invaded and covered Ra and settled down throughout the country and covered all the ground until it was black. They devoured all that was left after the hail—everything growing in the fields and the fruit on the trees. Nothing green remained on tree or plant in all the land.

In the morning Pharaoh summoned Moses and his brother Aaron. Hannu and his ministers watched as Pharaoh bowed his head in supplication as they had never seen.

"I have sinned against the Lord your God and against you," Pharaoh said. "Now forgive my sin once more and pray to the Lord your God to take this deadly plague away from me."

Moses turned from Pharaoh and walked into the bullrushes where he could not be seen. Then the wind slowly changed direction, growing from the West and the locusts were blown against buildings and people. Hannu's back was pelted and he knelt and covered his head then stood up and watched the black cloud flow into the desert.

Hannu and all of the people watched as the sky cleared and the wind stopped. He took a deep breath, looking to his Pharaoh who also watched, standing tall and proud. This man, this man-god, this Pharaoh will not allow it, he will refuse yet again. His heart sank as Pharaoh spoke.

"The skies are clear, your God has hurt us all he can, what more can He do? You and your Hebrews shall remain under my dominion which is the dominion of immortality. Heed my words, Moses, make your people understand what your cruel God has done to Egypt and we will forgive them and take them under our strong arms and bring them to truth."

Chapter Eight – Darkness

A thick murmur ensued, punctuated by moans and cries. Pharaoh was not a fool nor cruel to his people, but he continued to subject Egypt to disaster and the fear of what would happen next made the people shudder. He must, Hannu knew, be convinced to allow them to leave but how does one convince one who is descended of gods? Or might the words of Pharaoh convince Moses to stop his own God? Did Pharaoh believe that would happen?

Hannu thought of his son, Paneb, who had spoken few sentences in two weeks most of which foretold disaster; was he speaking in metaphor? Had he also touched immortality and spoken truly of the future? If the Hebrews were to turn to Pharaoh would the death Paneb foretold still happen?

Pharaoh stood among his ministers, tall and straight before his people. No words were spoken as all eyes were on Moses whose hair ruffled gently from a breeze no one else felt. Some gasped as the breeze grew to wind that whipped Moses' robe and his hair beat his face. His eyes opened wide then closed to angry slits as he looked at the sky and lifted his hand.

Darkness. Thicker beyond the deepest night, a black cloud enveloped the land and nothing could be seen. The murmurs of fear erupted into horror. Hannu lifted his hands to his face in vain, he could see nothing. There was only a gentle light over Moses and Aaron as they walked away, then all was blackness.

"My Lord, Pharaoh, please, I must speak." Hannu spoke to Pharaoh's direction as his guards tried to light lanterns.

"Say not what you will, you know not my plan."

"What is your plan? Is your plan the death of Egypt?" Hannu yelled into the darkness, his insolence lost to him in the horror of this new plague. "You are a man-god, touched by immortality yet we suffer under your words and decisions."

"I will hear none of this!" Pharaoh yelled, "Have him seized!" But the pitch darkness kept the capture from occurring. Hannu dropped and crawled among the panicking people, some legs kicking, others tripping over him, cries everywhere. He passed the palace and rose and felt his way, building to building, stumbling into terrified people dashing and crawling through the streets. These men and women were used to fear but they shivered and bold men screamed and drew weapons upon each other.

He finally found his house. Feeling the low wall, he walked to the door which was barred. He knocked then pounded, hoping it was his own, fearful of meeting a stranger or even a friend who would address him with a weapon. Finally, he heard Paneb's voice.

"What do you want? We have nothing, leave us!"

"Paneb, it is your father."

His son opened the door, reached out and pulled him inside. Paneb then closed and barred it again. In the house all was darkness. Hannu asked him about Chiome and Lapis.

"We found each other in the garden, they are hiding there."

They made their way to the garden and Hannu called out and Chiome answered quietly. Lapis was with her, she assured him, they were together. The dark night was marked by screams and words of anger in the streets that did not stop. Hannu shepherded them to the master chambers upstairs; in such darkness there would be lawlessness, let them ransack the first floor, he could defend the second.

For three days, as the darkness imprisoned them, they stayed in the master chambers, stumbling occasionally into the kitchen to find food. Hannu had gathered his weapons and set them by the door. He thought of taking his family to Goshen where, he was sure, there was light. He had blasphemed against Pharaoh, what would the god-king command? Perhaps they could live among the Hebrews. But how to find his way in such darkness? And could he subject his family to such a journey? Pharaoh would punish Hannu of course but would spare his family, he was not a cruel man.

On the fourth morning a red dawn bloomed over the desert. Hannu rose and watched as it blossomed and Ra opened the sky to them once again. It was Ra, he knew, was it not? This was the sun god crossing the realm of Horus, opening up the world for all people, not just Hebrews, to live in. But the God of the Hebrews, wasn't He the cause of the darkness? Where were their own gods, all powerful, benevolent, and helpful to their earthly children and the god-king they favored?

As he saw his family to their quarters, quietly glad to see the sun rise, Hannu knew he must go to the palace and supplicate himself. His blasphemy before Pharaoh shocked him; his thoughts of doubt were shameful. How could he imagine going to live with the Hebrews; to worship this cruel and deadly god of theirs as if they would even accept him? His sleepy Lapis still whimpered as she had for the days of darkness; if she had slept at all it was fitful and rare. Now he carried her to her bed in the morning quiet and laid her down.

"This will never be over will it?" He was happy to see her sweet eyes again, tired, and red as they were.

"I think so, soon, my jewel," he said, "I go now to help to end it."

"I hope you can, father, I know you can."

The streets were littered with moaning wounded and silent dead. People were rushing to find their own, frantically looking at every corpse, seeking loved ones. Others tended to the wounded or mourned. Hannu knew he was blessed to have his family safe, now he must make himself safe with his gods and god-king.

Pharaoh had already summoned Moses when Hannu arrived so he walked to his place among the court as if he had not blasphemed. For the moment he was unbothered and watched as Pharaoh descended the ramp. When Moses entered from the anteroom he was bent and hollow eyed and leaned on his staff while Aaron stood tall and his face was angry and he wielded his staff like a weapon. They stood in the entrance to the court and waited.

"Go, take your people," said Pharaoh, "all of your people, your women and children as well as men, and worship your God and leave us in light. Only leave your flocks and herds behind lest we suspect you are leaving forever."

Moses said, "You must allow us to have sacrifices and burnt offerings to present to the Lord our God. Our livestock, too, must go with us; not a hoof is to be left behind. We have to use some of them in worshiping the Lord our God, and until we get there we will not know what we are to use to worship the Lord."

Pharaoh stepped past his guards and walked across the court slowly. He stood close to Moses, half a head taller in his finery.

"I ask you to end this," Moses said, "it is in your power, your people suffer through what you cause them to endure, your deceit rains horror on Egypt. Please, I am asking you."

Pharaoh's eyes widened and he rose with expanded chest and said "Get out of my sight! Make sure you do not appear before me again! The day you see my face you will die."

Moses nodded. He turned to look at his brother and the anger that was on Aaron's face overcame Moses. Turning back to Pharaoh his words were heated. "As you say. I will never see your face again."

"Then leave me!" Pharaoh thundered.

"First hear this!" Moses stood close to Pharaoh and looked suddenly as tall and spoke in anger.

"We have performed these many wonders before you, before your officials and magicians and you have suffered and observed but your heart is hard and you have no mercy for your own people so I say this to you; You must let my people go now or you are warned that every firstborn son in Egypt will die. From the firstborn son of you, Pharaoh, touched, so you say, by immortality, to the firstborn son of the female slave at her hand mill, and all the firstborn of whatever animals you still have left as well. There will be loud wailing throughout Egypt; worse than there has ever been or ever will be again but among the Israelites not a dog will bark nor a baby cry. Then you will know that the Lord makes a distinction between Egypt and Israel. All these cowering officials of yours will come to me, bowing down before me and saying, 'Go, you and all the people who follow you!' After that I will leave."

Moses turned and left. Pharaoh stood watching him before turning away. Hannu bowed his head; was his son, Paneb, touched by immortality to know his fate? Did the Hebrew God give him a sign? His own blasphemy was no longer important.

"Hannu."

Hannu looked up, Pharaoh was looking at him.

"Leave."

Chapter Nine – Goshen

It was late morning and the streets were clearer as Hannu walked home. Most of the dead had been removed. Some lay wrapped in rags as cabbage or lettuce leaves were nowhere to be found, but none lay unattended. Mourning cries flowed from windows and doors, some prayerful and others abrupt and wrapped in pain. The door was not barred and he entered the silence and walked into the ruined garden. The dead fish lay in the pond, ripped vegetation floating among them. The soil in the gardens was pale and empty, traces of green and roots visible but nothing lived through the hail. It seemed so long ago, that storm that had been the tragedy of the ages.

He sat on the stone bench. The dead fish must be removed or they will stink. He would direct his servants. He must have the garden replanted, the garlic needed so much time this late in the year, how would they get a crop before Pachons, the month of harvest? He rose, paced the garden. Where there was no roof the walls and floor were pocked from the storm, they would be plastered and repaired. The grove of dead palms stood like naked poles, thick and without bark; they need replacing. He would bring in a team of gardeners.

How long had it been, days, weeks? He could not remember, even how many days of darkness they endured. Before that there were gnats; or were they flies? There were no flies in Goshen; he remembered the relief of riding out of the cloud of flies, the horses thundering before the chariot; were they retrieved? Did they try to go home when the flies lifted, only to die in the hailstorm? They fled and Qen died, for what? For Hannu to witness the destruction of his nation? Could he rebuild his world? Would there *be* a world? Would his son be a part of it? What could be done to keep Paneb alive? Was he powerless? Was Pharaoh powerless?

Everything Moses said had come to pass, why would anyone, even Pharaoh, think this latest horror would not? When the soft voice of Lapis rose behind him he was startled from his sadness.

"Father, do not worry, we can fix the garden."

"Yes we can, Lapis, my jewel, yes we can. We shall fix our world."

"Is our world broken? Did you end the horrors?"

He wanted to lie to her. "I don't know, I tried."

"If you tried as hard as you can than it should be fixed. You did your best."

He walked to her and picked her up and carried her to the bench, sitting with her in his lap. "I have such wise and wonderful children; the gods bless me."

"Except your son." She looked at him. "Paneb?"

"Yes," he smiled and nodded, "I remember his name."

"Oh father," she slapped his arm gently, "Silly. He is quiet and horrid and says nothing when I ask him anything."

"He is wise beyond his years and that wisdom weighs heavily on him."

"I would not be happy to be so wise."

"We are all wise in some ways, it is not a choice. Your brother is burdened, perhaps we can relieve it. Let us go and be with him."

In the morning the streets were clear as Ra made his way up from the east. There were few people about and no sounds save occasional sobbing. The darkness had taken its toll; the city was in restless despair. There had been no crowds to hear Moses' latest threat and Pharaoh's ministers had kept their peace yet the city seethed with questions; what will happen next? Could anything be done? The Egyptians now felt only fear. like children in the throes of emotion, they could feel nothing else. In the absence of any conflicting thoughts, terror was taking hold. Hannu walked quietly, listening, thinking.

As he entered the anteroom he stopped to let his eyes adjust to the dark then walked slowly in. Pharaoh was atop his throne, Hartumn stood beneath him, speaking quietly up to the god-king. Slowly the ministers noticed Hannu. As Pharaoh allowed himself to be dressed he turned to look at him. The brightening sky shone down into Hannu's eyes as he dropped slowly to one knee, bowing his head. Pharaoh looked at him in silence.

"I show restraint," Pharaoh's voice was loud and filled the court. "What is left in the storehouses shall be opened to my subjects. Wine and food shall flow in plenty and there will again be music and kindness in the sky."

Hannu hesitated and no one spoke. He looked up. "My god-king is wise and generous."

"Your blasphemy was under stress, your god-king understands. It is not beneath one touched by immortality to understand stress."

Hannu bowed. "You honor me." Relieved, he took a deep breath, looked back up. "My god-king, I would take a chariot and ride to Goshen, there must be things to learn soon, before..." He bowed his head.

"Before the next calamity, yes." Pharaoh was dressed and descended the ramp slowly. "What do you imagine can be learned?"

"Perhaps there is something that can be done."

"And you will learn what that is?"

"Perhaps. We must try, master, we must."

"And why you? Why would I not send out a dozen guards."

"No one would speak to them."

"They might speak to you?"

"Perhaps, if I show humility, I can find something out, some way, perhaps."

"I will send you with two guards."

"I must go alone, master, the Hebrews are tight with their ways, guards will hinder my search."

"Lately they have been not so tight." Pharaoh grimaced at his joke. "Can you control a chariot? It is not as easy as you may believe."

"I must try, master.

"My stablemaster, Nehi, has devised a way to ride more easily. He has made a saddle similar to those used on camels. He can show you how to use it, would be easier than a chariot. Go see what it is like and let me know your choice."

"Yes, my god-king." Hannu rose slowly, bowed, and turned to leave.

"The troop that went last week, they saw no sign of the horses you left, see what you can find."

"Yes, my god-king."

"Hannu!"

He turned.

"Tomorrow I send chariots to Goshen. No work is being done, the Hebrew men all left their places of work in the darkness, this must end. Find out what you will and come back to your family tonight."

"I will come back."

As a mare was being prepared with the saddle, Hannu thought about the words of the god-king. Barely veiled threats: an army was going to Goshen tomorrow to get the Hebrews back to work, come back to your family tonight. Was it suspected that he would flee? If so it would not be without his family.

The saddle was two yokes across the horse front to back with fabric stretched across that Hannu creased when he mounted. He was told to check periodically to make sure the leather thongs holding the saddle in place were tight. Nehi shrugged when Hannu asked how he should mount and dismount.

The mare was thick and slow and they left the city at a walk. Hannu had obtained a few supplies he thought may help including a vessel to fill with water so as not to have his horse defile their wells. The ways of the Hebrews were strange, what little he knew of them. There were certain foods, plentiful and delicious, that they would not eat. Osiris flooded the Nile annually so they could have food in abundance yet the Hebrews limited their diets. They were a strange people. Was letting a horse drink from their bucket unclean? Would that displease their God?

He was told they prayed as a group, all of them, not leaving such things to the priests as normal people do. How do you approach such people? How do you ask them questions? He had knowledge of use to them and they are men like Hannu and he was skilled in words. He had much to learn if he could get them to teach. There must be a way to save his son.

Once outside the city the mare seemed anxious and he let her trot then canter briefly, gripping the front yokes of the saddle as he bounced. The entire city was on edge, even the animals and why not, the goddess Hathor made all of her subjects sentient beings; didn't the horses buck before earthquakes? The past few weeks were like an abominable earthquake to Egypt, it made sense this mare needed to run some stress off. Slowing down to a walk they rode steadily for an hour when the lands of Goshen came into view. The sight, however, of that first village was different; instead of a quiet group of small houses, there was movement and men among the people walking busily about. Hannu stopped and dismounted by sliding off the side of the horse. He checked the leather thongs which seemed tight enough and led the mare toward them.

Women shepherded the children indoors at his approach while some men gathered on the road in front of him and waited. Far from humble, they stood tall and unafraid with muscled arms and swarthy faces. They said nothing. He retrieved the vessel from the pack and held it up as he approached.

"I would use your well to water my horse." They said nothing, opening up to let him pass he realized they were watching the desert behind him. "I am alone."

"Why would you trust us not to kill you?" One spoke and was immediately hushed by the others.

"I am a man, my horse needs water, is that a killing offense?"

"You are an Egyptian man." Again, he was hushed and he turned to those around him. "Why should we not confront this man? What does he bring that may harm us?" He was a short, young man, his robe light and off his shoulder in the Egyptian style but with the blue colors of Hebrews. His full, red hair was bright under the sun.

"I come in peace to beg water for my horse and knowledge if there is any to gain."

"You carry a khopesh!"

"There are threats in the desert."

"We have no knowledge for you, nothing. Water your horse and leave."

"Kefir be quiet!" An older man stepped forward, perhaps into his thirties with fine grey hair. "Go, water your horse but use your vessel. If we have knowledge for you we know not what it may be but we will decide whether to give it or not."

They watched him fill the bowl at the well and let the horse drink. Watching them as he sipped from his waterbag he wondered what would he ask them. These men are from the frontier of Goshen, should he move deeper into this land or be satisfied with what he could glean right here? He tied the mare to one of the palms surrounding the well. As he approached he held his head high. He would be humble but not afraid. There were eight of them, the older man who had spoken earlier stepped forward.

"I am Lior, what do you want?"

"I have ridden far, can we sit?"

Lior nodded and turned and Hannu followed to a group of rude benches of palm planks laid over mounds of mortar. As Hannu sat so did Lior at the other end of the same bench. The others stood.

"There were two horses, I was here with another a few weeks ago." Hannu was not sure how long ago it was, it could have been the day before the darkness came or weeks.

"You ride alone to retrieve some horses? This is the knowledge you wish from us?"

"No, it is not."

"I have your horses," someone said, "they are safe, we have no desire to keep them. If that is what you wish take them and leave."

Hannu turned to look at the man. "Thank you. I have more to ask but thank you."

"So, nu? So ask, please, we are busy," Lior said.

"Pharaoh will be sending chariots tomorrow. Work has stopped with the darkness; he will have it begin again."

"Yes, we expect as much. Being among our families again has been a blessing, one we know you cannot abide us having."

"I tell you in hopes that you can prepare."

"Prepare? He orders us to make his bricks without straw, something no man can do!" Kefir said, "He orders this so you can beat us. Have you felt a whip, then strained under a bucket in this sun? How do we prepare to be beaten like oxen?"

Hannu was silent.

"Would you like to see? Shall we show him, show this Egyptian who comes to help us? Is that what you are saying?" Kefir said.

"Kefir," Lior said but Kefir would not be silenced.

"Let us show him, this fine man, look at his robes. Have you seen a beaten man's back? Have you watched your father or child beaten?" He turned to the others. "Show him, show this man who would have us prepare for the armies of Pharaoh." No one moved. "I will show him."

Kefir turned his back to Hannu and dropped his robe. His back was laced with scars above and below his loincloth.

"All of you, let him know it is not just me, that I am not some special subject, let him see what his Pharaoh orders for us."

The others looked to Lior who stood up and dropped his robe and showed an equally riddled back to Hannu, some scars fresher than Kefir's. Then the men all turned and showed him their own scars and fresh slices across their sunburned skin.

"Oren, come here!" One man called. A boy walked out of a nearby hut slowly. "Come, show this man your back."

He was a shy boy, perhaps six or seven, wearing only a loincloth. His legs were bowed, his bare feet disfigured. He limped in pain to his father and looked up at him.

"Do it, show him your back, show him what his Pharaoh does to a child."

Oren turned around, trembling. Hannu could not speak. His vision blurred as he forced himself to look at the thin back of this boy, riddled with raised welts and strafe marks. There were fresh ones as well as many that were scarred and Hannu would have been unable to count them. What kind of man does this to a child, even a Hebrew child? Surely, he reassured himself, Pharaoh did not know of this and would stop it.

"Are those tears? Do you cry for us? Do you feel for us Hebrews as if we were actually human beings like you? Is that what I see?" He touched Oren and pointed him off and the boy stumbled on his broken feet back to the hut. "He was carrying mud when he was barely able to walk because your Pharaoh needed a granary or a house or a palace quickly. So, his legs are bent from the labor because his bones were not ready for such burdens and now his legs and feet can hardly carry him and because he walks slowly he is beaten. Beaten! Whipped! Have you watched a child being whipped? Have you watched your own child being whipped?"

Hannu sat shaking his head slowly. He knew of atrocities, as Second Vizier he had overseen roundups of Hebrews for projects requiring fast attention, is this what was caused by the haste he instilled, by the quotas he set? He knew the Hebrew supervisors were sometimes beaten to assure timely construction, he ordered it at times and gave it no thought. Was every Hebrew man, and even boy, beaten as well? This would be why the God of these people was so cruel to the Egyptians.

"We find you stupid, cruel and stubborn," Lior spoke quietly. "Moses has shown you what God can do and you suffer it and pay no heed. There is doom in your world now, as there always is in ours. Your compassion does not move us. What do you ask of us?"

"I ask if there is some way to save my son's life."

"Can you save my son's life?" Oren's father asked him. "If we remain in servitude to you I will see my son die. Or will your Pharaoh suddenly grow merciful?"

"Moses has foretold that the firstborn sons of Egypt shall die."

There was silence. They were surprised; Hannu had expected them to know this but it was obvious they did not. Three of them walked quickly away, the other few spoke among themselves. One bent down to speak quietly to Lior. He listened then turned back to Hannu.

"We have been told to prepare..."

"Do not tell him!" Kefir shouted, then lowered his voice. "Lior you cannot tell him."

"He is a man, he has a son, we must help him."

"We must not! He is an Egyptian. We cannot tell him anything. You endanger all of us, he already knows more than he should."

"Prepare for what?" Hannu grew anxious, he almost had it, almost had something. "How will you prepare?"

"Lior you cannot tell him!" Kefir said.

"They cannot thwart the will of God," Lior responded.

"They will try, you know they will!" Kefir said. "We have been commanded, he has not! You know what they will do, they will have time to..." He looked at Hannu. "Take your horses and leave us, suffer as we suffer, or beg your Pharaoh to bend to the will of God."

"Our gods do not threaten to kill children," Hannu said foolishly. He must better weigh his words.

"Your gods?" Kefir said. "Do your people not kill our children every day? Who cares for your gods?" He spit to the ground. Lior gasped.

"Do not mock the gods." Hannu rose and stood face to face with Kefir, his hand on the hilt of his khopesh. "Do not blaspheme lest you feel their wrath."

Kefir stepped back.

"What were you told to prepare?" Hannu turned to Lior who stood up. "Tell me what you have been told. I will tell no one. I come here not to thwart your aims, only to save my son."

"We cannot trust you," Kefir said. "We cannot speak against the will of God. Lior, we must go."

"Please, I beg you, if there is anything I can do to save my son, anything."

"Yearling lamb or goat..."

"Lior stop! You will get us all killed!"

"This is in the hands of God," Lior said. "It cannot be stopped, this man cannot stop it, all he can do is save his son, maybe."

"His son will not be saved. You cannot help him."

Lior turned to Hannu. "A yearling lamb or goat, male, unblemished. You must get one."

Kefir stared at Lior then turned and walked quickly off.

"Your God has killed all of our livestock," Hannu said. "We have none, no lambs or goats."

"Then your son will die."

"I will get one, I will find a yearling male, unblemished. Do I pray to him?"

"No, we don't pray to animals."

"Then what do I do?" Hannu asked anxiously.

"I do not know. I do not, you must wait."

"Wait for what?"

"I do not know. If God allows it you will be told what to do."

"Should I come back?"

But Lior turned and walked off.

Hannu found the other two horses tied with the mare. He must find a yearling, there are none in Egypt so he must find one here in Goshen and pray it does not die when he enters the city. Gathering the reins of the two stallions he pulled the mare aside one of the benches and mounted and rode deeper into Goshen, looking for herds. It was a green land, the streams that flowed from the Oasis of Sumat were rich and good to the earth here. Why had Pharaoh given this land to the Hebrews when it was so rich? He remembered the stories of Joseph, a Hebrew who grew in great favor to Second Necho years ago. That was before they grew into a nation and needed to be subjugated. Now they held this sweet land. Such suffering, still, is a heavy price even for this place.

He spotted a rude pen of reeds and willow and inside were several lambs and goats. He dismounted as the animals came to him, mewling for food. Most of the lambs were large and would be over a year although Hannu really had little knowledge of such things. He climbed the low fence as there seemed to be no gate. Cornering a young goat, he lifted and carried it back over the fence. He laid the small goat on the back of one of the stallions and secured his legs under the horse's girth. Then he laid a thin pale sheet over the animal to shield Ra's bright rays.

As he looked for a stump or bench to mount he saw faces in the doorway of a hut nearby. He wondered at the worth of the animal, perhaps two shat. What could he have that would be of use to these people? Ordinarily he would not think twice about simply riding off but these were not ordinary times. Would they use the bowl he had brought to water the horses? Having no idea what their God might demand of them he thought at least they could use it to water their animals. Hannu placed it in front of the gate then found a stool and mounted the mare. He left the goat on the stallion and walked them back toward the first village.

The village was empty as he rode slowly past. As he approached where the wall of flies had stopped them days ago, he looked back. Lior was standing alone and lifted a hand, motioning Hannu to wait. Lior looked back then walked quickly to Hannu.

"Two sundowns from today you must slaughter the lamb at twilight."

"You said a lamb or a goat."

"Yes, a lamb or a goat. Roast it over fire, head and entrails and legs and all. But before you roast it you must do this." He looked back at the village; no one, it seemed, was watching. "Take the blood and put it on the top and sides of your doorframe, do you understand? Then roast and eat it quickly with your cloak tucked into your belt, your sandals on your feet and your staff in your hand. What you do not eat you must burn, all of it must burn. Be careful to do this all and your son may live."

"Put the blood on my doorframe? Is that what you said to do?"

"Yes, do that. Do that and your son may live, do exactly what I said, now go." He turned to leave, Hannu watching as he took a few steps then turned around.

"You must try to understand," Lior said, "it has taken these few weeks, seeing these plagues fall on you, to begin to believe that God was going to finally help us. You have not known bondage, you wear the robes of a nobleman, it is easy for you to believe in your gods. But we have felt deserted and finally realize, most of us, that we may be freed. You cannot imagine how it feels to finally know this, that God has mercy on us."

"Is that how your God shows his mercy to you, by destroying us?"

"You destroy yourselves. You know this, that is why you asked for help. You are powerless before God..."

"Before your God."

"Before God. You are powerless and you know this. Whatever you worship is not protecting you."

"Did your God not allow that child to be whipped."

"Is there no pain in your world? No suffering? This is the way of man no matter who he is."

"Why do you tell me this?"

"I have children."

"And this will help save my son?"

"We do as we are commanded and God commands these things of us."

"That you eat this lamb quickly, in your sandals, holding your staff?"

"Yes, those things, and more."

"Of what good are they?"

"I don't know."

"Tucking my cloak into my belt? Why?"

Lior shrugged. "It is commanded. Perhaps God has a sense of humor." He stared up at Hannu. "Understand this; the blood we put on our door frames will show God where the Hebrews live and when He takes the firstborn sons He will pass over those houses."

"If He is a God how does He not know this already?"

"I only hope, for your sake and the sake of your son, that He may not know everything. I wish you hope, I have lost two sons, I do not wish that evil on any man, even you."

He turned and walked away. Hannu watched and quietly said thank you.

Chapter Ten - Passover

Put the blood of this goat on the frame of his door, how strange were these people? He rode slowly. This God of theirs, it seemed, demanded much of them. The gods of Egypt served the people, this God of Hebrews commanded and demanded they serve Him. Noon was past and the day had grown hot but the animals were watered and there was no rush. He slid down to check on the goat who was panting. Untying the legs, Hannu lifted the animal off the stallion, holding it tightly as he placed it on its feet. He tied a line gently around the neck of the animal but there was no need, the goat followed him back to the mare and waited patiently as Hannu gripped the yoke and pulled himself up. The goat found what little shade was created by the mare and walked slowly in it. Hannu lifted his veil and rode, shaded, through the desert.

Seeing the city did not remind Hannu to watch the kid walk under the arch but no animal broke cadence and the train of three horses and a goat entering drew plenty of notice. Talk stopped or began quietly as they rode slowly past. Approaching the palace, people lined the road. In an earlier plague all livestock was lost and now this Second

Vizier to Pharaoh was bringing a goat from the desert. This would have meaning; in these dark days everything had meaning. As he rode toward the stable, Pharaoh stepped from his chambers at the opposite end of the palace from the court. He walked onto a small porch in a white robe enclosed by a belt of blue and gold beads. Riding to the porch, Hannu slid down and dropped to one knee.

"My Pharaoh, I return with the horses and a portent."

"Hartumn has been summoned." Pharaoh looked at him. The animals panted, knowing the journey was over. "Have the horses tended then come back to this porch, I will hear you in private."

At the stable the goat drank deeply from a trough as Hannu addressed a guard. "As I am a tool of Pharaoh you are a tool of me."

The guard dropped to one knee and awaited his orders.

"I am Hannu, Second Vizier to the god-king Pharaoh." The guard nodded, knowing full well who he was. "This goat is sacred to all of Egypt, bring him to my home safely at once and see he is tethered in the garden of my home. Tell whoever is there that I have commanded this."

"Yes, my lord." The guard rose.

"See to it at once and let nothing prevent this. Confirm a guard on this animal until I get there."

When he had refreshed himself, Hannu walked to the porch of his god-king where Pharaoh waited with Hartumn. They both sat on reed chairs. Hartumn looked stiff and grim. "You may sit."

There was a stone bench at the foot of the porch stairs and Hannu sat down. Pharaoh nodded.

"Begin."

"The Hebrews instructed me. We have two days to prepare. My god-king must forbid labor or beatings of any Hebrew children; this has angered their God. This command must be heard throughout Egypt within two days, every corner where a Hebrew resides this must become known as a law."

"Why did Moses not say this?" Hartumn asked. Pharaoh listened with interest but Hartumn was ready to pounce at any words. Hannu had dealt with him in this mood before.

"Moses made only one demand," Hannu said, "that we let the Hebrews go to celebrate their God for three days. He asked or demanded nothing else."

"And why did he not?"

Hannu shrugged, shook his head. "I do not know. I did not speak to Moses."

"To whom did you speak?"

"I spoke mainly to a man named Lior but also to some others."

"What others?" Hartumn was not going to let any question go unasked. While he was technically a superior to Hannu, he rarely acted as such although Hartumn did enjoy the benefits of his office. There was typically no ceremony between Hannu and the sem-priest but Hannu had blasphemed and now sat at the foot of Pharaoh's porch while Hartumn sat next to Pharaoh.

"I spoke also to a man named Kefir."

"And why should we believe Lior and Kefir?" Hartumn turned to Pharaoh. "The names of these Hebrews, they have no poetry." Pharaoh nodded, watching Hannu with a small smile as if amused.

"Because they did not want to tell me. I asked their indulgence, asked for help."

"Help with what?" Pharaoh asked.

"Help with keeping my son alive. Moses said the first-born sons..."

"*Do you think your god-king does not remember what Moses said*?" Hartumn spoke from his seat.

"I was asking for help, to keep my son alive. My boy, Paneb, he is entering manhood, in his fourteenth year. I fear for his life."

"Do you not believe that your Pharaoh will keep your son, and all the first-born sons of Egypt, alive?"

"I beg Pharaoh's indulgence, this was a way to gain sympathy, mentioning my son."

"And what did they tell you to do?"

"I brought home a goat, a yearling, unblemished. I have had it taken to my house."

"Yes," Pharaoh said, "I have been told."

"Tomorrow night I shall slaughter this yearling. I shall do so at twilight then I will eat it in ritual."

"What is the ritual?" Pharaoh asked.

"I am to eat quickly, wearing sandals with a robe tucked into a belt and holding a staff."

Pharaoh squinted then smiled and looked at Hartumn who took the liberty from this glance to laugh.

"You must eat with one hand?" Hartumn asked.

"So it seems, yes."

"What purpose could this have, eating with a staff, wearing sandals?"

"I do not know."

"And that is all, that is the ritual? Nothing more?"

"Only that the entire goat must be burnt, entrails, legs and hooves, all burnt before Ra begins his ride across the sky."

"And you expect this to save the first-born sons of Egypt."

"I expect nothing, I can only hope to save them. If this manner or meal will do so I am happy to do it."

"This will save all of the sons or only yours?"

"I do not know. Their God also asks they have a day of rest tomorrow, I would humbly advise the chariots not ride into Goshen."

"You would advise this as Second Vizier?" Hartumn asked. "Or as a friend of the Hebrews?"

"I am Second Vizier to my Pharaoh and his servant," Hannu snapped, he was a humble man but not some commoner. "I am no friend of the Hebrews but even if I was I am neutral in all issues as much as my Lord The First Vizier."

"You have tried the patience of your god-king and you spout nonsense." Hartumn turned to Pharaoh. "At least, my lord, he has brought back your horses. I suggest a small feast tonight to honor the rebirth of Osiris. We shall recite lamentations as we eat this baby goat beltless, barefoot and with two hands."

Pharaoh smiled at this. "What is in your heart, Hannu? Did you pray with them to the Hebrew God?"

"I did not, my Pharaoh."

"Would you have? If they offered to save your son, would you have prostrated yourself with them and spoken in their tongue to their God?"

"I know that my heart would have been with Ra and Osiris and my god-king had they asked me to pray."

Pharaoh clapped his hands three times and a scribe walked onto the porch from inside the palace. He knelt before Pharaoh then backed down the stairs and set a pot of ink and a scroll on the bench next to Hannu, then sat. Pharaoh waited as he lifted a reed brush and dipped it in the ink.

"We shall have a feast tonight for the city from the stores we have saved. Hannu shall have his ritual."

"As you wish, my Pharaoh," Hannu said, looking only at Pharaoh.

"We shall hold the chariots from Goshen for a day. We shall see what happens if we indulge the Hebrews in this manner."

Hannu felt his heart thunder.

"It shall be known that Pharaoh does not permit the labor or beating of any person under the age of puberty. We do not condone such violence; it goes against the will of Pharaoh and Ra."

The scribe scratched hieratics into the papyrus.

"Now go, see to this at once."

The scribe rose, gathered his goods, and backed away. Hannu, sensing the end of this meeting, slipped to his knees and touched his forehead to the ground.

"Now go."

At his home Hannu walked into the garden to see Lapis leading the goat slowly around the wreckage of plants. She was talking to him gently and letting him munch noisily on the bits of vegetation available. Hannu had feared this happening, that she would think this a present to make up for her lamb who had died in one of the plagues. She saw him and smiled.

"He is Shu, father, like Tefnut and Shu, remember, the first pair of humans? He shall begin a new population of goats for us. The first goat, do you like the name?"

"It is clever, I like it very much." She was his sweet Lapis again, smiling and murmuring to the animal softly. Hannu decided to let her enjoy for now, everything was in doubt, give her this day as Chiome had given her a day.

That night Lapis played a discordant farewell to Ra before Hannu and Chiome dressed and attended the feast, leaving the children fed and attended by servants. Restless fear was visible in the eyes of the people who filled the palace yard. A small group of musicians with a female singer played soft, sweet songs of love and happiness that might have soothed the crowd had they been less anxious. Servants brought out bowls of roasted chestnuts, baskets of bread with garlic and dates and melons while people spoke quietly, suspect of the next moment. Plates of pigeon wrapped in lettuce were placed at tables of nobles but most platters had no meat. This lack, however, was assuaged by an abundance of beer of which people took great advantage. Still, the talk remained idle and the air seemed to shiver. When a glass or plate was dropped some were startled and called out or fell to their knees in fear.

While beer was typically drunk several times a day, this drink was from Pharaoh's own brewery, rich and stronger than most and eventually more than a few stumbled.

Emboldened and freed of anxiety by the drink, many went back for more and the pavilion on which the vats of beer were placed lay puddled with foam. There was finally a laugh, then another answered and they were so out of place in the melancholy gathering that people stopped and glanced toward the welcome sounds. A few smiled wistfully, as if remembering similar acts, and tried to make such mirth happen in their own conversation. As more people overindulged words became slurred and loud, punctuated by forced laughter.

Hannu kept Chiome close, sitting at the table with some other nobles. Across the table sat Khufu, Pharaoh's First Vizier and Hannu's superior. He was an old man who, while somewhat clouded, treasured his vaunted role and eyed the youth and will of Hannu jealously. Khufu had not appointed Hannu as Second Vizier, Pharaoh had done so as a favor to Hannu's father. This broke with tradition as Khufu had planned on appointing his own son who sat next to him drinking yet another glass of beer. Pharaoh kept Khufu as Vizier but paid more and more attention to Hannu's advice. Now Khufu, who had lost his wife years ago and sat as if his son was not there, looked across the table at Hannu and spoke.

"I am told you visited the Hebrews today; that you have information that may save us."

What little conversation that was happening at the table stopped. Some looked pointedly at Hannu while others, mostly spouses of the ministers, looked down at their plates. Hannu opened his mouth in surprise, glad he had sipped only a small bit of the brew. The noise of the crowd ebbed and flowed as if riding a tide, first loud and strident then soft and guttural.

"Do we need saving, my lord?," Hannu replied.

"Do you see the people, Hannu?" He took a long sip of beer. "Do you live among us? If you do not see a nation that needs saving then your eyes are closed."

Khufu's son looked now at his father, reached a hand to his shoulder. Khufu shook it off.

"Tell us, Hannu, what did the Hebrews tell you that will save us? We are all nobles here, we wish to know, do we not?"

He looked around the table but all eyes fell.

"Listen to the crowd," Khufu continued, "the fear in this city is strong. Perhaps we should pray to the Hebrew Gods?"

"They have only one God."

"Even easier, much easier than having to pray and make offerings to the dozens we enjoy, right?"

Hannu smiled and nodded. "Yes, much easier."

The musicians played the Pharaoh's march and the palace yard grew quiet. While all eyes turned to the Pharaoh's entrance, Khufu remained staring at Hannu. When Chiome noticed she took Hannu's hand.

Pharaoh entered with his guards. He wore a white robe belted by white silk; there was an ebony cone atop his head and a braided beard of gold at his chin. His sandals curved up luxuriously with each slow step as he crossed the yard. At the ramp to the dais the guards turned and faced the crowd while Pharaoh ascended slowly. He took his place before the lectern and looked out at the crowd before closing his eyes.

The yard had been designed for the grandfather of the Pharaoh who was a soft-spoken man. There was a wall of mortar coated with silver that ran behind the dais then turned straight ahead for a few cubits before angling outward. Above the dais was a sloped roof of the same material and paint, dropping down behind the speaker and rising slowly into the yard. Several of these walls with the same slanted roof stood at specific points through the yard. The result was that all in the yard could hear even the softest voice that rose from the dais. It was unbeholden for a Pharaoh to raise his voice; a god-king must do all with ease. He stood quietly, eyes closed, then raised his arms to the shining roof above him.

"My thanks for this milk of Heset, for this abundance of our river of Hapi which brings us our life."

The crowd responded, "We drink of the udders of Heset and the floods of Hapi."

"Drink deep of the udders of Heset." A goblet of beer was set in front of Pharaoh which he lifted and drank.

The crowd watched in anticipation. To whom Pharaoh prayed after this toast would signal to them the state of their world in the eyes of their god-king who, being touched by immortality, knew what the future would bring.

"It is said that if his heart rules him, his conscience will soon take the place of the rod."

He opened his eyes and surveyed the crowd, some sitting, some standing, all silent. This was unusual to begin a prayer with a proverb, surely there was portent in this. Hannu saw meaning that most did not and felt hope, squeezing the hand of Chiome. Turning to his table he saw Khufu still looking at him.

"Isis, awaken us." Pharaoh said.

"Awaken us," the crowd responded. A prayer to Isis would be for awakening, renewal. This was appropriate, all could understand this.

"Awake in peace lady of peace." Pharaoh recited slowly.

"Lady of peace."

"Rise thou in peace and in beauty."

"In peace and in beauty."

"Goddess of life, beautiful in Heaven where there is peace, beautiful on Earth."

Pharaoh had not said 'the Earth is in peace' which completes this line. The crowd hesitated then some began and all followed. "Beautiful on earth."

"Beloved of Nut, beloved of Geb, beloved of Osiris, goddess rich in names, all praise to you."

"All praise to you."

"I adore you, I adore you, Lady Isis." Pharaoh lifted the goblet.

"Lady Isis." All drank, renewal was foretold, relief should follow.

Pharaoh put his goblet down and descended the ramp where his guards again flanked him as he walked slowly to the palace door. When he was gone the crowd awakened with quiet talk.

"Now then," Khufu spoke immediately as if there had been no interruption, "shall we then pray to the Hebrew God who seems to have so much power? Or did you bring some magic back to protect your country?" Some of his words were slurred and his eyed darted from Hannu to Chiome.

"Khufu, my lord," Hannu rose as did Chiome, "I was told of a ritual which our god-king has permitted me to perform. As for you and the people, I suggest praying to the god of your choice, personally I prefer Ra."

"Who cares what you prefer?" Khufu rose, fell back to his seat then, gripping the table, rose again. He was a tall man but bent with age. When his son rose next to him to help him stand Khufu shook off his hands. "We are dying of fear, our world collapses around us and you perform a ritual? Where are the sem-priests? Where are those that are close to Isis that should be performing this ritual?"

"It was suggested to me, my lord, and our god-king has given his permission. Please pray for success."

"And what is this ritual?"

"It entails a sacrifice, and a meal."

"Sacrifice? Not of a human I hope." He chuckled then slipped and fell back to his seat. Still chuckling he looked around at the others at the table. "Who knows what we can expect of the Hebrews?" There had been no sacrifice of humans or even animals in decades, such doings were uncivilized.

"No, your honor, not of a human." Hannu took Chiome's arm and they left the table.

Out of the palace yard the street was quiet and the sky rich with stars. Chiome held her husband's arm as they walked slowly.

"His affection for you has not grown."

Hannu smiled and shook his head. "No, I have a long road to travel to enter his old heart."

"So does his son."

"Yes, I am afraid so."

"I feel sorry for him."

"Don't waste it on him, my love, we have trials yet to come."

"You are telling me how to spend my compassion? My wise husband?"

"You're a woman. You need direction."

She punched his shoulder.

"How was *that* direction?"

"That was quite direct." He rubbed it, shaking his head. They walked in silence. "Let us go admire the river."

Chiome nodded and they walked a short lane to a low wall. On the other side the shore sloped down to the Nile, low and shimmering in the starlight. The moon rose as a low crescent, the goddess Nut having granted it freedom only after its sacrifice to her.

"What of this goat?" Chiome asked.

Hannu sighed. "I must do this, the goat must be killed and eaten."

"Do you think it will work?"

"We must try, *I* must try."

"That is not what I asked you."

He turned to her abruptly. "Chiome I don't know, I only know I must try." He had not told his wife of the latest of Moses' threats, only that it would be devastating.

"So, we have to hope you can fool the Hebrew God?" She turned and looked out at the moon's shimmering reflection in the Nile. "This is our only hope?"

"I don't know if it's our only hope, only that I must do it."

"And Lapis? She loves that goat already."

"Yes, I know. I must break her heart."

"*We* shall break her heart."

When they arrived home Lapis was asleep on the floor of her room, the goat next to her, both wrapped in a blanket.

In the morning Hannu walked to the palace. Pharaoh had already said his morning words at the Nile and he sat atop his throne, dressed in a yellow kilt and blue and gold necklace. He sat unmoving; his eyes closed. Hartumn stood at the foot of the ramp, facing the throne, his eyes closed as well. Khufu, who usually did not appear at these morning sessions, was among the officials who stood, eyes closed, head up facing the god-king.

Hannu stopped and stayed very still so as to not interrupt this session of prayer. He thought of Ra, his deity of choice all of his life, and beckoned for his aid. He could not lose his son; it would be unbearable. He silently begged forgiveness for the Hebrew ritual he was going to perform that night. He wanted to believe it would work but these Hebrews were not simple, why should their God be? His deity Ra had not protected him, nor had the god-king or any of their gods; why would he not try anything? He pictured Ra, his hawk face and eyes filled with wisdom. Surely he could end this misery, could stop the latest threat of Moses but so far he has not. Could this be a punishment from their own gods as well as the Hebrew God? He saw again the back and legs and feet of the boy Oren, beaten and broken; would Ra have permitted this? Pharaoh was sending out riders to all corners to make sure this beating of children is forbidden; will that bring Ra to their aid? Perhaps, along with the sacrifice to the Hebrew God, they could save the first-born sons of Egypt. Or all of Egypt.

Hartumn broke the silence, his words ringing out boldly.

"Thou made a Nile in the underworld.

Thou bring forth as thou desire to maintain the people according as thou made them for thyself.

The lord of all of them, wearying with them,

The lord of every land, rising for them,

The Aton of the day, great of majesty."

"Great of majesty," was repeated by all. Hannu opened his eyes.

Pharaoh rose and began descending the ramp. He spoke as he walked. "We have sent chariots to all corners of our land to note there will be no harming of children of any creed, Hebrew, Egyptian, Nubian, all children under the age of puberty will not be touched nor forced to work."

Pharaoh spoke staring straight ahead at Hartumn who stood at the foot of the ramp.

"A ritual will be performed tonight; I command patience and prayer. All subjects must be aware, they must seek the help of their deity and god-king to assist in the ritual. See to that now. All but Hartumn leave as we will spend this day beckoning our gods to come to our aid tonight. The day is holy and full of hope and portent, treat it as such."

As Hannu walked home the criers were already out ringing their bells three times between chants; declaring the day holy. People took note, some stopping and standing with closed eyes as the criers passed, silently evoking their deity's aid; others rushing off to begin their prayers in silence and solitude. Hannu felt proud of his people, so quickly ready to create a holy day. It gave him heart and faith that the threat of Moses would be avoided. Surely the gods would listen when all of Egypt showed such piety and faith.

Once home Hannu set a place for a large fire in a corner of the garden. He was heaping wood when Lapis walked in, holding the goat on a leash.

"Shu and I bid you good morning, father. Are we having a fire? Will there be a feast for this holy day?"

"Good morning to you and Shu, Lapis. I am sorry to tell you that Shu must leave us, he was only to stay for a day. I am sorry, my jewel, I will get you another."

"But I don't want another, I want Shu." She began to cry. Hannu took a deep breath.

"There are children with much less than you have, Shu has been promised to them, he will be happy and spread his happiness."

"*He is happy here and makes me happy*!" She stomped her foot in anger and the goat jumped.

"Yes, I know, but this is foretold, I am sorry. Say goodbye to him, we will get you another as soon as we can."

"*No!*" She turned and stormed off as Chiome walked in.

"Leave her," she said, "I'll get him, you prepare. I have asked Paneb to help you, he will come down shortly."

When he appeared Paneb was dressed in finery Hannu had not seen on him in months, a belted tunic with multicolored panels of red, blue, and green covered by a sheer kilt from his hips to his curved sandals. Hannu smiled.

"You look all the man you are, Paneb."

"It is a holy day, father."

"Yes it is, and I prepare for a feast tonight, but a feast for only one."

"Only one?" Paneb asked. He stood near his father, looking taller than Hannu remembered.

"You have grown, my son, so quickly."

"Father, only one for this feast?"

"Yes, only one, me. I have been selected for this ritual by our god-king."

Paneb grimaced. "He will have us all die."

"*Paneb, do not speak such blasphemy!*" He put the piece of wood he was holding in the pile, then sat and looked at his son. "I have been selected by one who is touched by immortality to prepare this feast in the style of the Hebrews. The nation is praying today to our deities to help us end this... this disaster that has befallen our nation. You can help by joining, Ra hears loudest the voices of the young."

"It is to no avail, father, but I shall pray."

"You must believe or your prayers will not be heard."

"I will try, father, I will try."

'This is all for you', Hannu wanted to yell to his son, 'I will blaspheme against my gods tonight to keep you alive.' But he said nothing as he walked to the pile of logs and picked two up, placing them carefully among those already stacked so that they would burn hot and even.

They worked in silence for an hour, assuring the logs would stay, laying a thick layer of tinder at the base. When Chiome walked in she had the goat on a leash. She looked at Hannu.

"You must get this goat out of here now."

Hannu nodded and walked to take the leash.

"This animal dies for nothing." Paneb said.

"Paneb, why would you say that?" Chiome shuddered, tilting her head as she looked at her son. "We *must* take him from Lapis. Don't make this harder, please."

Hannu gave his son a glance and Paneb nodded to his mother.

"I am sorry, I am out of sorts. Was not ready for a holy day."

"You certainly look ready," she said, "now go to your sister and comfort her."

He nodded and walked off.

"What was that look you gave him, what does he know?"

Hannu shook his head gently. "He knows nothing. He seems to believe he can see things, events, in the future. He is a child; a bit melancholy is all."

"More than a bit," she said, looking at the door Paneb had exited through. "Perhaps he does see, perhaps he can help."

"He cannot help, leave him be, let him pray with his sister as we shall pray and prepare for the night." He took the leash and led the goat out of the garden.

Concerned that someone might hear the animal and steal it, Hannu secured the goat in a small, shaded vault next to the house where none could see or hear it. It was a cramped space and he wished he could provide more comfort for this animal's final day, but there was no other way; it must be hidden from all eyes, *especially*, those of Lapis.

Next to the vault was a boat that had been fashioned into a wagon by Hannu's grandfather. Spoked wheels rode on thick axles that had been drilled through the lapstrake sides. For years Hannu had kept the wagon in good repair though he had not used it since Paneb was born. The servants of his grandfather filled it with seeds and crops in those distant years but now there was no need; Hannu's fortune derived from the favor of Pharaoh as had his father's. He checked it over, felt the wheels and spokes, picked up and pulled the yoke; it moved easily. There were no oxen left in Egypt, he must use horses.

He cleansed himself then dressed in the white and blue colors of Isis, unbelted; he would wear a belt later during the Hebrew ritual. Chiome, too, was in white and blue with a headdress of silver and, as he evoked Isis and Ra she sat quietly. Typically, such prayers were performed by the sem-priests, individual prayer was rare except on occasions when people would follow the lead of the priest or Pharaoh. So Chiome was uncomfortable sitting with her husband as he prayed, unable to evoke her own deity, Wadjet, snake goddess of pregnancy and motherhood.

Hannu spoke out alternately from Isis to Ra, asking forgiveness then for help and she wondered what form of harsh reality did they need forgiveness for? She had done nothing wrong, nor had her children or husband as far as she knew. She did not question Hannu's words but if he had done something requiring mercy she was not aware of it.

She had lived a good life; her children were treasured and proper, smart, and polite and this was her doing, Hannu being gone all day every day in service to the Pharaoh. Now her family and her nation suffered through no fault of her own, her family was innocent of any wrongdoing. What Hannu did as he performed his duties to Pharaoh she was not aware. She watched him as he sat chanting and wondered.

"The god Tem, the Governor, the only One among the gods, hath spoken, and his word passed not away..."

She closed her eyes again and thought of Wadjet, pictured her coiling body writhing in ecstasy at the touch of Horus. Chiome had never chosen this deity, Wadjet was ordained to her by her day of birth on the eighth day of the month of Mesori, the spring solstice. If she had been able to choose her own deity would she be able to pray with more belief?

He finished and took her hand and the day of prayer was consummated in their bed. The gentle sound of Lapis crying pervaded her thoughts as Hannu entered her and was moved toward Ra and Isis. He must have heard his daughter as well but ignored it or was so humbled and in such throes of pious ecstasy that the sounds did not inhibit him.

Hannu *was* deeply saddened by the cries of his daughter but his duty to the people of Egypt and his god-king enabled him to finish this day of prayer by coupling with Chiome regardless. He was not his own man anymore, now he was the healer or savior or some kind of hero to his people. Without his invocations and the ritual that lay ahead of him the people of Egypt were doomed, as was his son. If forgiveness was ever needed by the people of Egypt, it was now. He fell into restless sleep as she lay listening until Lapis finally stopped.

Chiome then rose and walked into the garden and tried again to evoke her deity. The destruction surrounding her, the dead trees, the floating debris in the pool, the floors still pocked from the hail, allowed her no peace to concentrate. She rose and walked to the stack of wood Hannu had prepared for some odd ritual he would perform alone while his family remained upstairs. Under no circumstances, he ordered, were any of them to come downstairs. He would take them out of the house and bar the door if need be but he trusted them to remain upstairs; the fate of their nation could be at stake.

Dusk approached as Hannu rose, the house quiet around him, Chiome probably asleep with Lapis. He walked to his closet and removed the khopesh. It was, in fact, a ceremonial sword with little weight. He had never deployed it as a weapon but he was a strong man with thick arms and he had sharpened the curved blade to a fine edge. He assumed there would be no issues with this slaughter.

The goat rose and blinked and squinted then neighed nervously as Hannu walked into the vault and closed the door. Hannu laid a wide vessel of wood beneath the animal's head then raised the Khopesh. The animal looked at him, seemingly puzzled, so unaware of violence that it did not move as he brought the curved blade quickly down on its neck. The blade struck bone and stopped and the goat fell, it's eyes wide in terror and pain. Quickly Hannu brought the blade back up and, stepping over the animal, sliced again this time at the underside of the neck and blood pumped quickly into the bowl.

Pouring some of the blood into a smaller vessel, Hannu grabbed a brush and walked out of the vault to the door of his house. It was near black now, the low crescent of moon barely visible. He immediately dipped the brush in the blood and began to spread it over his door frame. He quickly ran out and refilled the vessel again and yet again to cover the dry wood around his door that soaked the thick liquid up. It was dark and hard to tell but he believed he had covered it all.

Lighting a torch, Hannu walked to the vault. Blood no longer trickled from the half-severed head of the goat. He wrapped the dead animal and carried it into the garden then placed it next to the prepared logs. Silence filled the house. There were four posts of green palm around the fire onto which Hannu lifted the copper rack his servants used for roasting. It sat firmly and, brushing flint to tinder, he sparked the wood with a low, gentle flame that rose quickly among the prepared wood.

The instructions were to roast this animal entrails, legs, and all, with no direction as to whether the animal should be gutted first. He used his khopesh to open the animal and remove the entrails, then he sliced the legs off, opening the joints and cutting the sinew. His heart pounded as he sawed and hacked at the neck, sweat dripping onto the dead flesh and the ground. When he had severed the head he coarsely skinned the animal, revealing sinew and muscle as he peeled back the skin first from the body then from each leg. When this was finished he placed the dismembered goat on the copper rack, entrails dripping into the fire. Then Hannu stepped away, cleaned his hands and arms and found his belt, sandals and staff against a wall where the greens of his garden had grown.

Donning the belt, he felt tired and alone. How long must this roast? How would this possibly do anything? Had he raised his own hopes and those of the Pharaoh with this foolishness? Was his son really in any danger? Things had been calm and quiet of late, perhaps if they left the Hebrews alone it would all pass. He sat down in front of the fire, staff in hand, curved sandals on his feet, and wished for an answer. Should he pray now? Would this ritual enrage Ra and Isis and all the other gods he had worshipped? *Could* it enrage them if the god-king allows it?

Thinking it better not to pray, he sat in silence, hearing only the fat dripping onto flames. He rose to turn the parts occasionally, most holding up but some of the entrails seeming to dissolve into the flames when touched. The scent of the burning fur filled the garden and rose into the stars.

When he felt the time was right he brought down one of the legs. He must eat in haste so he stood up, gripping the leg with one hand and the staff in the other, and bit. It was tough and tasted like charcoal and game but he chewed and swallowed and bit again. He was not told to stand but felt it proper somehow and he remained so, ripping off bits with his teeth until they ached and he could barely chew any more. His arm grew tired holding the leg to his mouth but he lifted it again and took another then another bite, unsure when to stop; it was not as if he had an appetite to satisfy. After a few more bites his stomach grew tight and that had to be enough; should he vomit up what he had eaten it might ruin everything.

He lay more wood on the fire then grabbed remaining portions of the goat and lay them into the fire; it must all be consumed. The copper rack glowed red atop the fire in the darkness as he added more wood around the goat parts. After a while he could see no sign of it anywhere in the fire. He made sure to leave access to the garden then barred the front door and walked out.

The streets were dark and empty. Where a month ago the lane may have been filled with mirth and the sounds of evening joy, now all was quiet; Egypt was in mourning and dread. He walked quickly around corners he knew well even in the dark. There was an entrance to the palace stable that most were not aware of and Hannu used the shy light of the moon to find it. Often there were guards at all hours, horses being wondrous things, but tonight there were none; all of Egypt was preparing for calamity, praying. Had Hannu run into a guard he would have used his office to ward off any questions and demand help. But there were none and in the darkness he opened the first two stalls. When the horses were awakened they snorted and whined but were easily quieted and he closed the doors before leading them out of the stables and to the street. He was grateful to leave the stone walks of the palace and reach the road where the hooves made softer sounds.

At his home he brought the horses around to the garden entrance and tied them to a post, laying a vessel of oats down to keep them quiet. Rolling the cart, he pulled it to them and lifted the halter, placing it softly on their necks then swinging the underside below and latching them together. This was correct for an ox, he hoped it would work for these smaller, weaker animals.

The dread in the air sunk into him as he walked back into the garden. When he went up the stairs to Paneb's room he was surprised to hear the rhythmic breathing of sleep. If the ritual works his son will awaken in the morning, if not then perhaps he won't; either way there was no more Hannu can do. He found the woven chair where Paneb would sit and look out at the river and he sat quietly. He would remain awake, watch over him so he'll know when it happens, if it does.

There was just enough light to watch the Nile shimmer and race toward the sea. His thoughts of gods gave way to the obvious power that the Hebrew God wielded then flowed quickly to Ra and Isis and his god-king, all powerless. The god-king, a man, even Paneb had said Pharaoh was not the man to protect Egypt in these times against this power. Moses asked only that his people be free to leave for three days but that was too much for the god-king, he could not permit it, his belief in his power prevented it. But what kind of belief could he have now? There was no majesty in his being anymore; he was too weak to realize how weak he was and it would doom them all.

The soft breaths of his son gladdened him and he watched the stars reflect in the water, the real god of Egypt, this river that kept them fed and comfortable and powerful; powerful enough to enslave the Hebrews and powerless to withstand the workings of their God. Was their God answering their prayers? These people who had watched their children beaten, didn't they deserve this vengeance on their enslavers? How cruel was this God? He had given Pharaoh a chance to release them which he could not take. Three days was all that was asked, a greater man would not have so jealously guarded his control over such an enslaved people. Now this God punished the god-king, punished them all by showing His power which even Hannu had laughed at.

Whatever happened to his son, this life was over. He could only hope the future held good fortune for him and his family. If he lived Paneb would be fine but he worried for Chiome and especially Lapis. The tiny bit of moon disappeared and even the stars found the darkness too strong. They dimmed and faded and he closed his eyes to them.

The long, quivering wail that woke Hannu was from a man, rising in a horrid crescendo before erupting into staccato cries searching for breath. As he opened his eyes pulsing moans echoed from other parts of the city and the cries turned to wailing again that slid into oblivion. A horn sounded disaster and Hannu could not hear if his son were breathing. The horn was joined by others and Hannu knew that Pharaoh's son was not spared. The cries increased from all directions, surrounding everything and he heard Chiome cry out then Lapis.

"Mother, mother, father what has happened mother..."

Chiome cried out then ran to Lapis as Hannu rose; Paneb did not move. The cacophony of cries from the city pierced Hannu's heart and he shivered as he rose then knelt at the side of his son's bed; betrayed. The Hebrews were not giving him any salvation, it was the darkest of tricks to let him hope. He heard Chiome trying to quiet Lapis as the city raged outside. Tears overcame him and he put his hands on his son's chest; his entire body shaking.

"What is wrong, father?" Paneb asked. Before Hannu's eyes could open he jumped back kneeling, straining to see his son's face in the darkness. Then he laughed, the relief so great he could not control it and his laughter drowned the sounds of horror from the room and he fell to his side and covered his face in his hands as Paneb sat up and wondered at his father and the grave noise of the city.

"Father," Paneb said, sliding from his bed to kneel next to Hannu, "what has happened?"

Hannu was sobbing richly and he reached out his hand to his son's. He could not speak. Chiome and Lapis cried out then followed the sobs to Paneb's room.

"We are here," Paneb cried out loudly and they heard him and rushed so quickly to the bed of Paneb that they stumbled over Hannu. As Chiome and Lapis settled hugging on Paneb's bed Hannu felt for and found his son's face and kissed him.

Paneb took his father's face in his hands. "Disaster has struck?"

"Yes, my son, yes."

"And I am spared?"

"Yes."

Hannu held Paneb then reached for Chiome and Lapis and his arms wrapped his family together as the screaming cries and horns of mourning of Egypt filled the air. The Hebrew God had spared them, the blood of the goat had caused His angel of death to pass over this house, he was truly blessed by this God.

He rose quickly and held them close to him as he spoke.

"We must leave now, immediately, there is no time to gather any but the most essential, we have short minutes. We must go together to each room to cloth quickly. This is no time for finery, dress for comfort."

"Where are we going?" Lapis asked.

"We must leave, now."

He walked them to Lapis' room and she dressed, then Chiome. Paneb was already in his cloak and Hannu led them quickly down to the garden, stopping in the kitchen to pack some slices of smoked meat, hedgehogs roasted in clay, lettuce, and garlic. In the garden the coals were still glowing in the truly sacred fire. Rushing past it he led them out and seated them in the cart. Leading the horses now to the street, he prayed that Ra did not rise any time soon. Of course, it was not Ra, only the sun that would eventually brighten the sky. But now it remained black and he climbed into the wagon then snapped the reins.

The horses were used to pulling chariots and not heavy wagons and they writhed under the oxen yoke. Hannu snapped the reins but they only reared then dropped down hard, yanking him forward. He had not grabbed a whip at the stable and did not think it would do much good anyway.

"Everyone stay still," Hannu yelled to be heard above the unending din.

Handing Paneb the reins with instructions to hold them loosely, he dropped to the ground and tied a leather thong to their yokes. Tugging gently, he led them from the yard, speaking softly to the horses though the cries of the city drowned his words and continued to unnerve them. Still, he spoke as he led them into the street, telling them how they would be saving lives by walking under these yokes and that he would honor them forever.

The darkness was waning and progress painfully slow. When he tried to hasten them from such a slow walk the yokes slid up the horses' necks and they lifted their heads and shuffled. At this rate he would be passing the palace as the sun rose; even under such duress the guards were sure to see and stop them. They had to ride, there was no other way. Neither his wife nor daughter had ever been on a horse and Paneb only briefly but there was nothing to be done.

He led them away from the palace then doubled back along a quiet lane hidden by the reeds of the Nile. Crossing behind the palace he stopped the cart along the river and called Paneb down.

"There are saddles inside, we must find them."

"Yes, father, what is a saddle?"

"What you have seen on camels to permit you to sit on them. We must ride and cannot ride without them."

"On camels?"

"No, on horses, we must put them on the horses, now come."

Entering the stables Hannu kept Paneb close in the darkness and walked toward the corner from where he had seen Nehi bring the saddle he had ridden to Goshen. Praying to every god he knew of and the One that saved his son, his heart rose in relief as he found and lifted one. Paneb put out his hands and carried it out to the horses as Hannu took another.

Untying the horses from the cart they tied on the saddles quickly. He helped Paneb slide up and helped Chiome down from the cart and up behind her son, laying the packs on their laps. Handing Paneb the lead line Hannu told him to hold them short and follow him. He then lifted

Lapis onto the other horse, handed her another pack then used a stool to climb behind her, silently praying to the God of the Hebrews. Leaving the cart and a few packs that lay in it, he led them to the street, grateful when the horse's hooves moved more quietly on the dirt lane though the sounds of mourning drowned even the darkness.

They rode slowly until a vague light shone on the gates of the city and Hannu quickened the pace, glancing back to make sure Paneb was behind him. When they did arrive at the gate Hannu stopped and waited.

"We must make haste now, you comfortable to speed up?"

"Yes, father."

"Chiome?"

"*Hannu! You waste time, go!*"

"Lapis, hold on."

He kicked his horse and they trotted then thundered into the desert. The darkness was deeper than in the city but he could hear Paneb and Chiome close behind.

Out of the city the grinding hooves of the horses were the only sound. Hannu slowed to a walk, letting Paneb catch up. After a few minutes Lapis turned her face to him.

"Father, I am scared, what is this? Where are we going?"

Hannu took a deep breath, looked behind them. Morning broke timidly.

"The God of the Hebrews has slain the first-born sons of Egypt, all of them, there is barely a house without death in it right now, not even the palace of Pharaoh."

"But not me?" Paneb said as if this might be a dream.

"No, not you, my son, the Hebrews showed me how to keep you alive. Such a deep sleeper." He smiled and laughed gently.

"What is funny?"

"When the city awoke with grief you just lay there sleeping. I was terrified, then you woke and I was more terrified. I almost jumped into the Nile."

The tension broke for a moment and they laughed except Lapis who stared, eyes wide with comprehension.

"By now Pharaoh has sent for me when he should be sending for Moses and demanding the Hebrews leave. We can no longer dwell in Egypt; our home now is among the Hebrews."

"I do *not like the Hebrews*," Lapis said.

"Have you even *met* a Hebrew?" Paneb asked her.

"*Silence from you!*" Lapis said. "I want to go home."

"This is not a choice, Lapis, they have helped me to keep my son alive when all of Egypt has lost theirs. The God of the Hebrews has shown that He is truly the one God. We shall find refuge with them and learn their ways and always thank their God for keeping us safe."

"No! I don't want to! I want to play my flute and bid Ra good night then welcome him in the morning."

"Lapis," Chiome said, "all of my life I have prayed to a god I never understood or chose."

"*I do not choose this one! The Hebrews, they are pigs and slaves*." She spit to the sand as she had seen done before by elders including her father.

"I never chose mine..." Chiome began.

"*I am choosing mine!*"

"*Listen to me!*" Chiome spoke harshly, "I was given my goddess, Wadjet, the serpent. I have prayed to her all of my life yet she was powerless to hold off the power of the Hebrew God. Now we are shown, your father has shown us what real power is, we shall follow."

"*I do not want to follow!*" She was crying as she tried to slide off the horse. Hannu grabbed and stopped her.

"If I go back Pharaoh will have me killed, *this is true*." He held her shoulders as she sat limp in front of him. "This is my family, Lapis, all of us. I will not sacrifice my life and put you and your mother and brother in danger because you act like a petulant child. There is a time for everything and it is now time for you to become a woman and do as you must. Is that clear?"

She said nothing.

"Remove your ideas of the Hebrews. Remember only that they saved your brother's life. More than that you will learn."

"Father? Can I turn around?"

He lifted her, she was light as air, as if a goddess herself, and turned her around on the horse to face him. She put her arms around him and nestled into his chest, sniffling. He held her as he looked back toward the city. The sun was high enough to make out the gates in the distance.

"We must go," Chiome said, "they will come after us."

Chapter Eleven - Exodus

Pharaoh sent no one after Hannu. The grief of the city grew through the night and he rose in dread and went directly to the chamber of Heqaib, his eldest son. Barely eleven years old, the divinity in him was not mature enough to fight off this Hebrew God. Pharaoh carried his dead son down the stairs and into the court, ascending the ramp slowly in the quiet light of oil lamps that shimmered in the vaulted room.

When he reached the throne he sat heavily, his son across his lap.

"I will see Moses." He spoke quietly. There was a guard in the anteroom but Pharaoh was alone in his court and no one heard him. "I will see Moses," he said again, louder but his words blended with the noisy sorrow that surrounded the city. Then he said it louder than the god-king had ever spoken. The guard, obedient and loyal even in his own immense horror, ran into the court and looked up at him.

"Summon him," Pharaoh said, quietly, "summon Moses to me."

The village was loud with action that had begun well before the first light. Grim faced women cooked and stacked thin loaves of bread over smoky fires, men loaded carts and children got underfoot in their efforts to help or avoid helping. There were donkeys and even goats hooked up to some of the carts but most were rigged to be pulled by people. The noise level was high but not strident or angry. Directions were called out and contradicted.

"Load both carts."

"Who is going to pull the other cart?"

"What do you need that third robe for?"

"How else are we going to cook?"

"God will provide."

"Like He provided our pots?"

Orders had been given and they moved quickly, determined to follow those orders to a better life. But no one was celebrating.

It was the children who first noticed the riders approaching and their words and cries were hushed before the adults looked up and saw them. Some shrugged and a few of the men walked warily to the front of the village. As the horses came into view there was some relief; two walking horses, even with four people riding, was no attack.

Lior was stacking bread on a rack when his daughters ran back to him and pointed the riders. They watched him as he looked up then walked quickly through the crowd toward the riders. Wondering what he was racing to, his family and others followed but stopped at the edge of the crowd as he walked toward the riders then broke into a trot. When he was close enough to be sure it was Hannu he stopped and started laughing and swaying with sweeping steps and raised arms, wrists snapping to the sky.

Chiome stared and held her son tightly as they stopped the horses. Her husband lifted Lapis in his arms and slid with her off the horse. He put the child down as Lior came closer but Lapis' hands stayed around his neck and Hannu rose with her holding tightly as Lior reached out and grabbed the sides of Hannu's head and leaned forward.

"I am *so glad*," he said into Hannu's face. He looked down at Lapis who looked up from her father's neck then hid her head quickly. "So happy to see you."

"Thank you," was all Hannu could say, his heart choking, Lapis holding him tightly. "Thank your God."

"Yes, thank God." He turned to the village as they watched. "*Thank God!*" he yelled. "*How wonderful is God!*" He turned smiling and looked at Paneb. "How wonderful," he said quietly.

He smiled at Chiome. "So beautiful, such a beauty are your children." He laughed. "And horses, you come with horses." He brought his face in close again and Hannu thought he would kiss him. "You have eaten? Of course not, come." He turned and Hannu and Lapis followed, leading the horse. Paneb dismounted then helped his mother down.

Everyone watched.

"He is now us; *they* are now us; *they are blessed by God!*" Lior yelled to them.

They slowly got back to work, some smiling, most wary and shaking their heads.

"You know where the spring is," Lior said, "go water your horses and yourselves and we shall see about food."

"We have brought food," Hannu said.

"But you must partake of our food, will you not join us?"

"We will not impose."

"Impose? Ha, we are all able to eat God's bounty, come."

Lior led them to a table of thick gopherwood, rudely cut on heavy legs. An older woman with thin red hair approached him and he took a few steps away from the table with her. They spoke quietly.

"Right now?" Lior said to the woman loud enough to be heard. "They just arrived, just got here, this can wait."

She glanced at Hannu then said something quietly to Lior, who sighed and nodded. As he walked back to Hannu he rolled his eyes.

"I am afraid," he said, glancing back at the woman walking away, "there is a ritual that must be performed."

"We have our own food, Lior, we are grateful for yours but..."

"You will not be a Hebrew if you don't do this. It does not concern food."

"We hope to leave with you and become Hebrews, what must we do?"

"You must be circumcised."

Hannu laughed, turned to Chiome then back to Lior and smiled. "That is not an issue, we are both circumcised, it is the way of Egyptian nobles."

"Ah, that is good news but is it complete?"

Egyptians were comfortable with nudity and Lior had seen overseers relaxing naked if there was shade so he knew that their circumcision removed only the outer membrane and left the corona. Hannu had heard of the ritualized circumcision of the Hebrews that removed the entire foreskin which the Egyptians considered not only unnecessary but cruel. They eyed each other. Hannu shook his head.

"Perhaps not but, can we follow you? We will eat only what we have and see to this ritual when we are out of Egypt."

"Of course!" He looked at the woman who stood watching them and raised his hands, nodding then turned to Hannu. "We only wish you to understand what is required of you." Hannu nodded and Lior broke into a broad smile. "Can we keep you from following? Only God can keep you from following. Sit and eat. Your food or ours, you are welcome."

The family sat. Hannu opened the package of food and lifted out a clay wrapped roasted hedgehog. He broke the clay gently on the table surface then opened it slowly. As he lifted the pieces of clay the spines stuck to it revealing soft, roasted meat. Chiome opened leaves of lettuce and scooped some of the meat onto them then added some garlic, rolled them up and passed one to each of them. The hedgehog had been soaked in vinegar before roasting to preserve it and the smell mixed with the garlic and rose from the table. As they ate they did not notice the crowd trying to prepare but unable to ignore the food. Finally, Kefir, the man who would have had Lior withhold the lifesaving ritual from Hannu, took a step toward them. Hannu looked up; when their eyes met Kefir walked closer.

"Your feast is pungent and exotic to us," he said, "to flaunt such food is cruel."

Hannu looked around as he realized what was happening. "We flaunt nothing; we mean only to eat."

"You eat what we have never even seen, what we have never been allowed to find or cook. Do you think your overseers permitted us such meals?"

Lior walked over. "Kefir, leave them alone, let them eat."

"If they are going to feast as Egyptian nobles they should partake where the smell will not tempt everyone."

"Just let them finish," Lior said.

"We live on bread and they feast, look at them, while our children stare they dine!"

"Are you hungry?" Hannu said. "Have you eaten?"

Lior cut Kefir off. "We are always hungry. There is never enough to make us full, only to keep us able to work. But finish your meal, we must begin."

"Have these children," Hannu asked, looking around, "have they eaten? Have they ever had meat?"

"Some salted fish, perhaps," Lior said.

"Chiome," Hannu turned to her, "bring out the rest of the lettuce. Lapis help your mother." He turned back to Kefir. "We have more hedgehogs, we will prepare them all."

"We do not need your generosity, only some manners," Kefir said.

"Your children are hungry."

"Our children don't need your food."

"But if they want some they are welcome." He lifted eight more clay balls from the bag and Lior and Kefir watched as he broke them open and scooped out the meat. "You see, we soak them in vinegar before coating them with clay and roasting them. The spines then stick to the clay, see?" He held up a piece of the clay. "Mixed with some garlic they are very tasty, come, try some." He offered them two filled leaves.

"Give them to the children," Kefir said.

"Yes," Lior agreed, "but first I must taste this."

"Take a small bite, these may be rich food for you. Maybe too rich for the children."

Lior took a small bite and chewed slowly. "Sweet *and* sour at once, strange. Kefir, take a bite."

Kefir took a deep breath, pursed his lips and took one. "You soak them in what?"

"Vinegar," Hannu said, smiling, "it preserves them."

Kefir took a small bite and shook his head. "It is like nothing I have ever tasted." He took another small bite then handed it back to Hannu who shook his head.

"You finish that," Hannu said, "we'll make smaller ones for the children."

As Hannu opened the other clay balls Chiome began laying out more lettuce leaves.

"We must put very little in each leaf," she said quietly. "If these children have never had meat it will be upsetting to them."

"Yes," Hannu agreed, "make them very small, more lettuce than meat. We can add barley."

"But that ruins the taste," Lapis said.

"These people have never eaten anything like this," Chiome said. "You saw that, but they are hungry, make them small and add the barley."

They rolled and handed out over a hundred, each with a taste of meat but hopefully not enough to upset the children's stomachs. Lior saw to handing them out while Kefir stood aside, finally speaking to Hannu.

"You have no concept of who we are, of what our lives are, or God."

"We will learn. We are learning already."

"You need more than generosity."

"Kefir," Hannu said. "I have a concept of your God, of God. I know that my son rose this morning as so many in Egypt did not. I have witnessed this miracle. I know we have much to learn but do not think we have no concept of God."

Kefir nodded. "I must finish." He walked away.

After they had eaten and handed out all the food, they rose and watered the horses again. The crowd slowly finished packing then sat waiting on their packs or carts.

Some of the adults paced nervously, some spoke quietly among themselves but the children ran playing and laughing. Hannu watched them; this was a solemn, momentous time for these Hebrews; in such a time in the city the children would have been hushed and made to sit quietly. Here they were free to laugh and play.

Looking into the crowd he saw the father of Oren, the beaten child, speaking with several other men. Telling his family to wait there with the horses, Hannu approached the man who saw him coming and turned to him as did the others.

"I know only the name of your son, Oren, but I am Hannu and will follow you from this land."

There was a silent moment as he looked at Hannu as if searching for words. "I am Abner."

"God has allowed my son to live. He has given me a gift beyond any."

"This is not a miracle? God gives gifts?"

"A miracle, yes." Hannu lifted his hand. "I have my family."

"Yes, we all know."

"I have two horses. They are Pharaoh's and should be disguised somehow, but I would have your son Oren ride."

"I can carry him."

"Yes, you can, but I offer this humbly to lighten both of your burdens."

"He cannot ride," Abner said, "no one here has ever been on a horse."

"My son rides, Oren will ride with him. He will be safe."

Abner looked at him and nodded. "Thank you."

Hannu walked to his family. "Paneb, there is a boy that cannot walk, his legs are too weak, his feet deformed, he will ride with you." Paneb nodded. "Go to that man, his name is Abner and give him the respect you give any elder but introduce yourself as a man, do you understand? You will be respectful but equal." Paneb nodded. "These are new times for us, you are no child, we will dwell with Hebrews now and you will make your way. Go ahead. His son's name is Oren and he has never been on a horse and will be nervous. You have to help him.

Paneb looked at his father and nodded solemnly. "Yes, father."

Paneb led the horse to Abner who called over the boy. Chiome took her husband's hand as they watched.

"Much happened that day you were here," she said.

Lapis looked up at him. "Father, there must be other children that cannot walk. They can ride with you."

He lifted and held her tight. "Yes, yes, we shall help them."

Arranging themselves with the others, Hannu and Chiome rearranged the packs on the horses and prepared to lead them. Hannu was concerned that Pharaoh or his guards would see the horses and know them for Pharaoh's but there was little he could do. A blanket over the horse would do nothing, it would look as much a donkey as a camel.

He watched Paneb lift Oren onto the other horse, holding the rein tightly. The horse, Nubian trained and docile, did not move. When Oren was astride he looked around from his height with wide eyes then looked down at the neck of the animal then at his father, smiling shyly. Looking at Paneb who was smiling up at him, he laughed as Abner watched.

"Be careful up there," Abner said.

Oren's eyes darkened. "Will something hurt me?" He was quickly afraid and pressed on the back of the horse to get down, looking at his father.

"Stay there," Paneb said, "I am your friend, I will not let anything hurt you."

Abner looked at him, nodding gently. "Trust this man," he told his son, "he will not let anything hurt you."

Paneb climbed on behind Oren. He reached around him and took the rein. "Can you feel the muscles under you? This is a wonderful animal."

Oren carefully put his hands on Paneb's arms. "Does he have a name?"

"I suppose he does but I don't know it, we need to give him a new name, what should we call him?"

"Let's call him Oren!"

"What? But what if I get confused and try to ride you? What would happen then?"

Oren's eyes widened until he glanced over his shoulder at Paneb's smile. "No," Oren giggled, "that won't happen."

"You never know. Let's think about it, we have time, okay? Now let's go for a walk."

He walked the horse off as Abner watched then went back to packing.

Hannu had fashioned straps to run around their shoulders and foreheads and fitted one to Chiome then to himself. Lapis refused to mount the horse, insisting on a pack of her own.

"You take a child who cannot walk," she said with a furrowed brow and aged gravity, "I can walk, we have discussed this and it is settled."

Hannu resisted the urge to smile, respecting her seriousness. "Yes, of course. I am sorry, I forgot."

Paneb joined them and they waited with the others, facing the opposite direction from where they came, looking toward the heart of Goshen. The entire crowd became pensive, watching the horizon, ready and waiting.

"What are they looking for?" Lapis whispered to him.

"I do not know, but we shall look and wait with them. Be patient."

A spot on the horizon blurred as if a storm were rising with the dawn and the crowd began murmuring. Hannu looked around, anticipation was everywhere as the people nervously gripped their hands or tapped their legs. Some smiled and nodded to others, wide eyed. The storm showed itself slowly to be dust on the horizon, approaching with a soft tremor of sound. A child cried behind him and a woman began a laugh that was joined by others as the eye of the storm widened into a broad base that built like a wave; the rising dust sparkling like a cloud in front of the sun.

"They are people," Lapis whispered.

"Yes, they are people, many of them."

She took his hand. "Millions of them."

The storm spread as it approached, the sound building into the footsteps of a crowd, each to its own pace, determined yet easy. When the earth beneath them began to shiver, the horses lifted their necks and spoke but did not move. Hannu saw Paneb speak quietly to Oren as they watched from their high perch. He heard voices in the distance that blended with the footsteps then singing that was joined by some around him. Soon many were humming and singing simple syllables in rhythm; here da da da da da and there ai ai ai then any sounds that were inspired and there were tears as the approaching people, now visible as individuals, came closer.

Hannu looked down at Lapis. "This is freedom for these people, do you understand?" She nodded. "They have been slaves for years and years and now they will be free and they are happy and singing." He went to the pack still on his horse and brought out her flute. "Here, play with them to the morning, as you would have done to Ra. But now play to us and to these people who will be our people."

"I don't know these songs, I can't."

"You can play to their happiness, please, it will do my heart good, and your mother's."

Lapis looked at Chiome who nodded at her. "Go ahead, play."

She brought the flute to her lips and began the gentle lullaby she played at dusk to ease Ra's transition to the underworld. The notes barely rose above a whisper, still a few glanced over at her, humming and singing and Lapis gained some confidence and played louder. The approaching storm now called out to them in loud greetings. Words of welcome rang out among the singing as Lapis found some notes from the song that pervaded the air and joined in. More wordless singing and humming rang out and some walked to her and watched and listened and sang and smiled. Her notes had never sounded as sweet to Hannu or Chiome who watched in wonder as some men surrounded them and took each other's hands or shoulders and began moving in a circle, stepping high, stomping in rhythm, then kicking and singing and laughing.

Lior broke from the crowd and reached out to Hannu and took his hands, pulling him into the line as Lior sang with pieces of words and syllables then someone put a hand on Hannu's shoulder and he stepped then kicked with them as tears coursed through the dust on his cheeks. Humming as he danced, Hannu saw Chiome smiling at him in tearful joy as Lapis played rising onto her toes with closed eyes, then lifting her face and flute to the sky and playing louder. All at once the approaching crowd was among them and Lior turned to Hannu and took his face in his hands.

"*You have given me faith in God, you are a miracle,*" he yelled at him, "*your son is a miracle.*" Hannu could not speak. Lior was rapt. "*We would give you a name, a new name. I would call you Joshua, God is Salvation! You are my salvation!*"

Lapis played as the circle grew with more dancing and singing. Paneb watched with Oren sitting in front of him. He could see the welts on the boy's back even through the robe. He put his hands on Oren's shoulders.

"Your people are happy," he said.

Oren leaned back onto Paneb. "I am happy to be with you."

This was not like a wave Hannu had seen when visiting the great sea at the end of the Nile; this was the ocean. People engulfed the village and those who waited picked up their packs. Men loaded kneading troughs wrapped in fabric on their shoulders and others pulled wagons loaded with flat loaves and bundles. The children laughed and played in the procession, but as the adults shouldered their burdens they moved with deliberation and gravity; it had been foretold by

Moses and they had hoped and prayed. Now it was happening and their joy was replaced by fear and wonder.

Hannu mounted his horse and from his perch he could see more and more people; there seemed to be no head to this march nor anyone leading. He expected to see Moses and his brother Aaron but the movement of the crowd was so dynamic that no one group or person was among the same group from moment to moment and there was no leader marking their direction. They moved toward the city and the gates to freedom as one. The air was punctuated by the calls of livestock and he watched herds move among the crowd, calling out in fear at this mass of people and the thunder of their footsteps.

When he did see Moses, he was not surprised. Walking separate and burdened, Moses' cloak was so torn and faded that Hannu wondered that it even held together. He smiled at the humility of this man that had been such an arrogant and strong-willed child. His arrogance was gone, it seemed, but his stubborn will was no weaker than it ever was. He dismounted and gave the reins to Chiome.

"Stay here, I will be back."

Chiome nodded to her husband, preferring to accompany him but marking her spot.

"The table, the gopherwood table, that will be our landmark, come back to us." She did not want to lose him in this crowd of hundreds of thousands. He turned and nodded then she watched him walk to a tired old man at the edge of the crowd.

Hannu approached Moses slowly, unsure of his intent. "Moses," he said, stepping next to Moses at his pace. "Moses, I am Hannu."

Moses stopped and looked at him, leaning on his staff. He said nothing.

"I know you from the palace," Hannu continued, "from your youth and from these recent weeks."

Moses nodded. Hannu was at least ten years older but this man in front of him looked ancient.

"I remember you; I am sorry."

"I am coming with you. I have been blessed, the Angel of Death passed over my home, my son lives and we will walk with you."

"So many of God's people died, so many, I am sorry."

"It was not you; you were God's messenger."

"I wanted to fight Him. I did not choose this. So many people, so much suffering."

"You cannot fight God."

Moses looked closely at him. "I would have, I wanted to but I was too weak."

"You are the strongest man I have ever known."

Moses smiled and reaching out he touched Hannu's shoulder. "I remember my days growing up in the palace, seeing you watch me, strutting like a fool so I could make you feel small as if I had anything to do with it, with my luck or your position."

"I watched you ride, so fast, down to the river, jumping gates and walls, you were graceful to watch."

"But you hated it, watching me, right?"

"Of course, you were a kid who got lucky but me, I believed I had to earn my way." He smiled. "I was made Second Vizier because my father had shown valor and

Pharaoh rewarded it. It took me a long time to realize my own luck."

Moses smiled but his eyes were deep and sad.

"I have a horse." Hannu said, "I would be honored if you would ride it. The leader of the Hebrews should be astride a horse."

"God is the leader; I am only His messenger. There are others more worthy than me, go find them."

Moses turned and began walking again, slowly. Hannu watched as some walked past him, others stayed slow at his pace but none approached. He walked back through the thickening crowd. Paneb and Oren were still visible astride the horse and he walked to them and addressed his family.

"We shall offer this horse to anyone who may need it. Let us begin."

They moved with the people of the village, Abner staying close with his family to Hannu to keep an eye on his son riding with Paneb. Hannu led his horse and they walked, Chiome holding hands with Lapis. As they became engulfed in the crowd Hannu ceased thinking about disguising the horses; in this multitude he was no longer afraid of being noticed. He imagined the city being choked by this mass of people; would they skirt and avoid it? He knew the city; how difficult it would be for all of these people to move through it. But this was not his concern.

Lior walked to his side as Hannu scanned the crowd for someone to put on the horse. Hannu had expected to see other children hurt like Oren but the children he saw ran and played among the adults, occasionally being called back by a stern parent.

"When we go to the city," Lior said, "we are to ask the Egyptians for whatever they can give us, clothing or jewelry or gold."

"Why would we do that?"

"God has told us to, they will be glad to see us leave and will comply. Are there valuables you left in your house? Do you want to go back and get them?"

"This crowd will never make it down that narrow road."

"Can this crowd fit down any road? We will walk through the city however we go and God will guide us to the gate. You can go to your home if you want to."

"I suppose we would want to but we want to stay with the village, will you all join us?"

"Stop worrying, you are in God's hands as we all are now."

The people of the city lined the roads and paths as the Hebrews entered. The restless fear that had pervaded the city was gone; there was relief and some sad smiles in the faces of those who watched them walk past. Hannu expected his family to stand out in their Egyptian robes but no one seemed to notice them. People were bringing food and water from their homes, also bundles of clothing and jewels and handing them to the Hebrews who stored them in packs or on their carts. Hannu headed toward his own home and the people from the village flowed through the streets with him.

Paneb shook his head, there was nothing of his former life he wanted but Lapis enthusiastically plundered her chambers. Chiome and Hannu packed their jewels although both wondered what they would do with them in the desert. Bundling their belongings, they packed it onto the horse and left. Hannu looked back with his wife and daughter before turning a corner. It had been a good house, a good life although misguided and, in fact, one that condoned evil. That life was over, he did not regret leaving.

He walked now past neighbors who recognized him, neighbors who had lost sons and could now see Paneb atop the horse walking with them. Expecting venom, he slumped and raised the collar of his robe to no avail; he was recognized. Looking up he saw that most of the faces that watched him had no malice. Some nodded, some small smiles, a few even said goodbye which he answered with a nod.

Reshet, Hannu's former neighbor, strode out of his house and called to Hannu.

"You warned of flies," he said loudly, "but you let me lose my son." He approached Hannu who stopped. There was no malice in the voice of Reshet but his eyes shone. "You let Egypt lose our sons."

"I could not save them. I tried."

People were walking slowly past them, watching. Reshet looked back at Paneb riding with Oren.

"You saved yours."

"Reshet I tried but..."

"You saved yours!" His eyes shook as he choked but found words. "You let my son die, you saved yours." He turned and walked slowly back into his house.

Hannu began walking again.

"That is true," Chiome said quietly.

"I let no one die. God took them." In his distraction Hannu forgot the misery of these, his former people. He did not feel the incredible despair they endured, despair he was meant to share. These people had no rage, wanted no revenge as their hearts were filled with grief. "I did all I could do. There was nothing more."

There *was* more. He had saved his son. He could have told a few, or many, or all, would it still have worked? Could they have brought back a multitude of yearling lambs and goats? Would the angel of death have been fooled? How many might have been too many to save his son?

They took the road that he took every morning to go to the palace to do the bidding of Pharaoh. Lior and his family walked in front of him, greeted by people standing outside their homes. They asked for things and were granted whatever they asked for. Hannu wanted nothing from any of them.

As they approached the palace he wondered if God had hardened the heart of Pharaoh after each plague as he now softened the hearts of the Egyptians. There were times he was sure that Pharaoh was going to let them leave only to turn and subject them to worse and worse calamities. Why was it necessary to cause so much pain; turning the river to blood was not enough? Did an enslaved people need powerful signs to be made to believe? He did not understand enough about misery, the misery of the hopeless and enslaved, to answer his question.

Passing the palace, he was uneasy but there was no need, Pharaoh was not watching from among or above the crowd. The pace did not vary, all moved as one, streets filled then led to others and people were separated then rejoined with quiet smiles, moving on expectantly, confident that God would lead them together.

The sun was high when he could see the gate. Lior came back to him, smiling, pointing.

"Such a gate!" he shouted. "Such beauty, we are almost there, almost in the promised land."

The Gate was beautiful only because it was the end of their time in Egypt. It had a thick lintel of limestone painted with images of lions and other cats surrounding Pharaoh as well as overseers whipping slaves with curling lashes and vivid Hebrew pain. As they walked beneath Hannu looked up at the images. As second Vizier he had helped to design them, meant to reflect the greatness of Pharaoh. He shook his head and walked into the desert.

The children grew solemn and held tight to their mothers as they left the city. When they turned east Hannu was surprised, this was an odd way to leave Egypt although he did not know where they were heading. The road to Succoth led to the Sea, surely no place to flee Pharaoh who could change his mind at any time. If they head north through the land of the Philistines they could easily go around. Egypt had long since stopped concerning themselves with the Philistines who would not dare test the armies of Pharaoh, but perhaps they would not fear this multitude of Hebrews. Still, it seemed odd and wrong and he gave the reins to Chiome and told them to stay together, he would return.

He found Moses at the periphery of the procession with a bag on his shoulder that weighed him to one side. He was walking with a young woman who was gesticulating as she talked.

"I do not doubt God," she was saying, "but what will *you* have us do now that we have nothing?" She was a tall, thin woman with thick, dark hair who gestured as she spoke. "What good will Egyptian Jewels and gold do us in the desert? We should know where we're going, do you? This is madness, Moses, you can indulge your madness but should we?"

She turned to Hannu as he approached. "You'll get more talking to that horse of yours."

"Do you know me?" Hannu asked her, surprised.

"Do you think everyone doesn't see an Egyptian with a horse to carry his things?"

"I have wanted to offer the horse to anyone who may need it."

She stopped. Her eyes and lips were soft and easy but her nose welled up strong. "Look around, you see nothing? Are there a million people out there? You see no women carrying children?"

"I offered the horse to Moses."

"To the most bull-headed man among us you offer a horse? Let him carry those bones himself, he needs nothing but God." She looked at Moses, "I suppose we all need nothing but God!" She turned and walked away from both of them.

Hannu watched shocked as she walked away then he fell into step with Moses. "Is she not blasphemous?" he asked quietly.

Moses smiled and shook his head. "You have not met many Hebrews."

"No."

"We are an opinionated people."

"You cannot have opinions about God." Hannu was incredulous. "God is God, that is all, this is not open to debate."

"Everything is open to debate."

"No, not this, not God. I would not speak against God after the miracle I was given."

"Are you asking for a test?"

"I am ready."

"Be careful. You want a test you will get tested."

They walked for a bit.

"I want to ask you," Hannu said, "to offer my services if I may."

"You wonder why we go this way."

Hannu was surprised. "Yes, there are shorter ways. If we go north toward Shur I can speak with the Philistines. I have worked with them; we have a treaty."

"They have no doubt heard of these last few weeks, know that Pharaoh is happy to see us leave and that we carry some of the riches of Egypt. Do you think they will honor a treaty, or an Egyptian who has left them to join this band of Hebrews?"

"I could try. We head now to the mountains of Migdol, it will be a difficult walk."

"God will protect us; this is where He directs us. Look." He pointed to the sky in front of them. In the clear air was a pillar of cloud, white and shimmering as clouds do, billowing in high breezes. "We follow where God directs us."

Hannu saw the cloud, how had he missed it earlier? "But it will be difficult, there are children who will need help, the passes are steep."

"Then we must help them, your horse will come in handy, no?"

"Yes."

"Go now, find a woman carrying a child and help her."

"Can I help with your burden?"

"This is no burden."

"She said they are bones."

"Yes, they are bones."

"You carry bones with you."

"I keep a promise."

"A promise to the dead?"

"Of course."

Hannu wanted to ask, hesitated.

"These are the bones of Joseph." Moses said. "He led us into this land hundreds of years ago and asked that we take them when we leave."

"You carry the bones of the man who led you into a nation that enslaved you?"

Moses shrugged. "We made a promise. Now go help someone with your horse."

Lapis picked a woman walking with a toddler and an infant. Her name was Ayala and she was leery even with Lapis mounted behind the toddler. The child looked around in wonder for a moment then put her hands on Lapis' arms and leaned back into her. Lapis smiled and held her tight as Hannu walked them slowly along. Ayala's husband Saul carried a kneading trough wrapped in some robes and was grateful when Hannu offered to share his burden. As the man stretched his relieved back, Hannu saw welts down to his legs. The toddler riding with Lapis, his name was Judd, he would grow into a man never feeling a whip.

The trough was lighter than Hannu expected and he eventually tied it to the horse behind Lapis and shouldered Chiome's bundle so she could relieve Ayala and carry the infant. Paneb stayed close with Oren asleep in front of him. They moved slowly, the gentle hum of soft conversations barely punctuating the quiet desert.

When they arrived at Sukkoth they could see the low mountains of Pihahiroth in the distance. Setting up camp they spent the night. Hannu had wondered how his family would fare but Lapis curled up with Chiome and Paneb with Oren who had begged his mother to let him sleep with his new friend. Hannu lay awake, wishing they had gone further from Egypt, this was less than a half day's ride for the chariots of Pharaoh.

At dawn they approached the mountains beyond which lay the Sea of Reeds. Hannu had been through some of the passes of Pihahiroth that opened into the valley of the sea. It was a narrow range with low, pointed peaks that would be a difficult walk. They would make it but what would they do when they arrived at the sea?

After camping at Etham they began early the next morning into the mountains. There was some easily skirted desert scrub atop the lower peaks but mostly it was stone and soil, not as hard to climb as Hannu remembered. He and Chiome walked with Ayala and Saul who were traveling alone. Chiome offered to take the infant; Laban was a stout, loud little boy, and Hannu spoke up.

"I'll carry the baby."

Ayala gasped, Saul and Chiome looked at Hannu who smiled. It seemed like a good idea. He laughed as they looked at him. This was such a shock? It was not as if he never held his own children. This would be easy.

"I can carry my pack *and* the baby. You women can put your packs on the horse for a bit and walk unladen, it's a long, uphill climb."

"I'll carry my son," Saul said quietly, taking the baby from Ayala who stretched up and kissed him then looked at Hannu for a long moment before smiling.

As they rose to the higher passes the Sea of Reeds came in and out of view, stretching wide, horizon to horizon. It was a pretty sight but made Hannu wonder again where they were being led. At one rise Ayala and Chiome, who had taken to walking together, stopped and stared. Hannu had traveled to this and other lands in the course of his dealings but Ayala nor most of these Hebrews had ever seen anything like this. As they topped rises and hills and were able to see it they all admired this body of water in wonder, so much wider than the Nile, so blue and shimmering.

They began to descend and it was as hard as walking up and people sat on boulders to stretch their knees and legs. Eventually all arrived at the long reach of valley that led to the sea and walked south. Walking along the shore the Hebrews both enjoyed and were horrified by the sight and feel of the water. Gentle waves brushed a cool wind over the feet of the few who dared step in. Hannu helped Judd and Lapis dismount then held Lapis' hand as she walked in it, giggling. Saul held Judd's hand, watching wide eyed as Lapis walked in the water.

"He can try, hold his hand, you should try it too." Hannu said. Saul took the hand of his older son and walked to the water, glanced back at Hannu who nodded then stepped in. Judd giggled as soon as he stepped in and Saul smiled at him and laughed with his son. Lapis let go of Hannu's hand and kicked some water at Judd then Saul kicked some back at Lapis. People surrounded them, watching, uneasy about this huge sea and what may come of touching or walking in it.

Hannu was leery of removing his robe among the Hebrews, he did not want to show them his unblemished back. Keeping himself covered, he ran into the water up to his knees before diving in. He swam a few strokes before standing up, his robe clinging to him. The water was cool and soft to the touch and it washed off the sand and sweat of the last few days. He had hoped his example would embolden some of them but no one followed except Paneb. The Hebrews did not go in any deeper than their feet. Saul shook his head when Hannu looked at him. Of course, he realized, these people had never been swimming, had no idea. He looked at Paneb and motioned to go back.

"This is all new to these people," he said to his son as they walked out. "We must not expect them to follow our examples nor show them things they'll not do yet."

Word came that they were changing direction. Looking up, Hannu saw the pillar of cloud was north of them. There was murmurs of discontent as they turned and walked back the way they had come and some wondered if they would now go back over the mountains.

They did not go back over the mountains but walked north of the pass and arrived at a place opposite the gentle peak of Baal Zephon which loomed across the sea. Hannu watched as Moses walked up a hill and turned to the crowd. The crowd noticed him and grew quiet.

"We follow the Pillar of cloud that some of you have watched," Moses said, "It led us here knowing that Pharaoh will think we are lost and wandering aimlessly."

At the mention of Pharaoh, the crowd erupted. In the course of their travels most had assumed that they were safe now, all they had to fear was the desert. Now they were being told that they might be pursued as well. They cried out at Moses from the foot of the hill.

"Was it because there were no graves in Egypt that you brought us to the desert to die?" they shouted. "What have you done to us by bringing us out of Egypt?"

"Didn't we say to you in Egypt," others cried, "to leave us alone; let us serve the Egyptians?"

"It would have been better for us to serve the Egyptians than to die at their hands in the desert!"

Moses lifted his hands for silence then did so again and shouted to them. *"Do not be afraid. Stand firm and you will see the deliverance the Lord will bring you!"*

But they were afraid and held each other. Chiome and Ayala sat with the children who felt the fear even if not understanding. Hannu walked to Paneb who stood with Oren and his family, watching the crowd. He gripped his son by his shoulders and looked into his eyes and was glad to see no fear. They smiled and hugged.

As they stood watching Moses and the sea, wheels rumbled in the mountains. Dusk was approaching but in the waning light the Hebrews saw the line of chariots form above them, hundreds of them, deadly and ready to sweep down in a fit of carnage. They erupted again in recriminations and fear and Moses again raised his voice above theirs.

"I told you, do not be afraid. Stand firm and you will see the deliverance the Lord will bring you today. The Egyptians you see today you will never see again. The Lord will fight for you; you need only to be still."

The sun was setting quickly but a light rose above them even as darkness engulfed the mountains and the chariots of Pharaoh. Moses walked slowly down through the crowd.

"Of all people to follow, we pick the man who was raised by the Pharaoh!" One woman yelled at him. "You were always insane, wild eyed, unable to even talk! Now we are doomed." She fell sobbing to her knees and when Moses tried to help her up she sprung away from him. "Do not touch me, Moses, do not ever touch me."

Moses looked around. There was quiet now and the crowd parted as he walked down toward the Sea of Reeds. When he reached the shore, he stood looking out at the water lit by the pillar of fire above. Hannu watched as Moses' lips moved but said no words that Hannu could hear.

Then Moses raised both hands, lifting his staff, looking out at the sea and a warm wind rose out of the west and agitated the surface so ripples rose into waves. Holding his hand and staff up he leaned back his head.

"*Go*!" he shouted, "*go*!"

The wind whipped into Hannu's face and blew his robe and worried the animals and children. He felt Lior at his side.

"Go where?" Lior yelled to Hannu into the wind. "Is Moses insane?"

Chiome looked at Hannu then at Lior shaking her head.

"We are here with our children," she said, "if this is the way of God we must follow."

"Follow where?" Lior said. "Would he have us cross the sea?"

"Yes." Hannu said. "My friend, that is what he would have us do."

He walked to the edge of the water in front of Moses. The wind whipped drops into his face and robe as he stood and waited for a wave to lift onto his feet but none did. He took a step and the water fell away and he took another.

"*Wait, Hannu wait!*" Chiome was hurrying toward him leading a horse with Lapis. Paneb led the other with Oren riding.

"No," Hannu said to them, "No, stop, we must walk on our own feet." He walked to Lapis and she slid off the horse into his arms. Paneb looked up at Oren then at Oren's father Abner who was always nearby.

"He can walk," Abner said, looking at Oren, "Can my son walk?"

Oren did not answer but slid quickly off the horse and stood waiting.

Hannu took another step. The water fell away and they formed a line behind him.

"No," he said, reaching out to Chiome, "do not follow, come walk next to me." She took his hand. He turned to the others. "*Just walk in, God will take care of you. Just go.*"

They walked and the waters receded before them then Lior and Kefir and their families followed. With each step that should have been into what was now a low wall of water, their feet remained dry and they advanced slowly and felt the crowd following, hearing the wonder amid the writhing waters. Each step brought them deeper and walls of water rose next to them and soon towered over their heads. In the light that shown from the pillar of fire they looked at the walls and saw fish flee the turmoil. There were reeds and weeds at their feet that were thick and full of clams and strange scuttling creatures. Hannu felt Lapis' hand squeeze his tightly and he looked down at her wide eyes and grim set lips. She looked back up at him for a moment then back into the receding wall in front of them.

The gap widened behind them as others walked into the waters that opened before whoever approached and there was soon a wide lane of dry seabed. A trumpet rang out behind them with the Egyptian call to attack. A cry of fear erupted among the Hebrews who now began to hurry into the waters, following the others. Some panicked and tripped or pushed but they could only go so fast and they pressed where they could, looking back in fear as the Egyptians, engulfed in a deep fog, attempted to charge down the mountainside into them.

The attack halted. The chariots could not move as the ground was littered with large rocks and thick brush that stopped them in the hazy darkness. The Hebrews could hear the cry of the horses as the chariot wheels jammed and the confusion of the Egyptian army was palpable and spurred them on and soon all of them were in the sea, walking steadily.

As Hannu walked toward Baal Zephon he wondered who among the Egyptians he knew; certainly at least some of the commanders. Good men, all of them, would they enslave him should they follow and take them back? More likely he would not survive being rounded up and his family would be sold into servitude of the worst kind. The mountain rose in front of them and the divide in the waters opened and in the sharp light of the pillar they could see the dry path extend to the shore ahead.

Lapis held his hand tightly and he looked down at her again. She was watching the walls of water around them, one right next to them and the other now a good thirty cubits away. The fish fled the eruption but the action of the water and the thrashing reeds and sea plants were feasts for the eye. Holding his hand almost too tight, she was able to look around in wonder and giggle and she even did a hop skip over some rocks then shrieked at a crab.

Paneb held both his mother's and Oren's hands and kept looking from one to the other protectively. Warm wind whipped his hair as the Sea of Reeds churned and broke in on itself but did not intrude on their path through the water.

Oren stared at the bubbling tumult next to him until his crippled feet hit a stone or some strange weed of the sea or even a scuttling animal that seemed to look up at him in defiance before running off. He walked across small fields of stony plant like things, spiny and colorful but sharp and he stepped over or next to them carefully.

When a fish as large as a man, it's face toothy with dull eyes, pierced the wall of water, Oren stumbled. The hands of his friend Paneb and his father were not enough to keep him from falling into a stone leaf, red and spangled with tiny shells. As it broke under his hands his father lifted him onto his shoulders. Oren looked at his hands, cut and beginning to bleed and his heart sunk as pain grew in his fingers like sharp worms until it stopped. He watched the blood steam off his hands and the cuts cooled as if cleansed by soothing oils and there was no more pain. The giant fish watched.

"Father, I will walk."

"You are stumbling."

"I will walk, father, put me down!"

Oren's father and Paneb glanced at each other and, while Paneb smiled and shrugged, his father did not.

"I will not let you fall again," Abner said, setting him down on the sands past the small garden of stone.

Oren reached up and clung tightly to the hands at his sides and watched the huge fish in the wall of water. His bowed legs and damaged feet constricted his steps but the wonders of this walk hid any pain even as the wind pressed him back or pushed him forward. That Paneb was able to hold his hand and keep the horse calm and moving, was as miraculous to Oren as these liquid walls and his healed hands.

Oren stumbled but did not trip again. Other huge fish watched and pierced the water in groups with long noses and grinning mouths that made clicking noises as if laughing. Oren watched and grinned, looking up at Paneb and his father who both saw the fish and smiled as well. In this amazing torrent, among these fish noisy and happy and others brooding and toothy, he squeezed the hands holding his and felt his world broaden with his heart. He knew little yet of the faith that led him here but forgave whatever power healed his hands for not healing his legs and feet.

Hannu wondered at this miracle and the power of God and where this would lead them as they began walking uphill toward the end of this opening in the Sea of Reeds. Turning around, he could see all the way back; the Hebrews were all in the break in the sea which had grown wider as the crowd moved in. Then trumpets blared with an echo that bounced across the water and the hillside was dark with the Egyptian army, hundreds of chariots charging in formation. The Hebrews at the end of the line closed up any gaps, their animals crying in fear. He saw the chariots close ranks and pour into the break in the sea, closing the distance to the Hebrews quickly.

Then they were stopped, all of them, the charge choked off suddenly and the horses stumbled. Chariots fell with broken axles amid the reeds and rocks of the seabed and men stood grabbing their swords to run after the Hebrews. As they began to run their feet stuck in the sea floor which was now thick and treacherous mud. Hannu watched the Hebrews separate themselves from the Egyptians as the sun rose and the last of the chariots raced in.

Then Hannu stood watching the path fill with water as the Egyptians tried to outrace the oncoming flood. They could not, the water quickly engulfed them and the mud held them down so they could not rise as the sea reached its depth. Soon all of the chariots were engulfed and no Egyptian man appeared on the surface. A dry path remained for the Hebrews until they were all on land below Baal Zephon.

Chapter Twelve- Safe

The Hebrews fell panting onto the shore. Beyond a few cubits of sand, sharp stones littered the rest of the shore and they struggled on thin soled sandals or bare feet. Oren limped to the rocks until his ankles gave way and he fell to a seated position. He looked to Paneb but it was his father who reached down and swung him easily onto his shoulders.

"Paneb must lead the horse beyond the stones," Abner said, "I have carried you for years, this job is mine."

From the height of Abner's shoulders Oren watched as the Hebrews made their way slowly across the stones, Paneb among them holding his mother's arm as he let the horse find its way.

"Is it a boy horse or a girl horse, father?"

"I would guess a boy but that is only a guess."

Abner was right, the horse was a stallion, whose name, Death of Namart (shortened to Namart), commemorated the victory he had taken part in over King Namart's hordes who sided with the Hittites and were dispatched by Pharoah's army. As much as the horses of Egypt were beloved, so were the horses of Namart's kingdom mistreated. When freed from their bondage, the horses of Namart were brought to fine stables the god-king ordered built by Hebrew slaves where they lived in well-kept luxury.

But Namart was not a horse bred to work or even carry riders, none of the Egyptian herd were. They were coddled animals who were massaged regularly, given wide stretches of desert to exercise and fed carrots and treats as well as the available forage. Their work consisted of pulling chariots into war or carts of Pharaoh's ministers afield. While Nubian trained and therefore docile, Namart was not pleased with this lack of amenities nor this new duty. He had never felt any animal on his back and now there were usually two and, though it was not a struggle for him, it was not comfortable. Walking slowly over the stony beach, picking up and carefully placing hooves used to soft sand, he was also hungry and his discomfort was evident to Paneb who spoke softly to him. The trauma of the walk through the waters added to the animal's stress and he shuffled and slipped and finally fell forward to his knees.

Paneb saw that the horse was hurt and his reaction was to reach around and caress Namart's neck and face but the injured animal bit his arm then rose, cried out and reared angrily. Paneb held the rein but let the animal have his lead, staying back as the horse stayed on his hind legs for a miraculously long time, screaming with front legs wheeling to the sky.

Hannu was already working his way past the stones with the other horse, a black gelding named Hebny which meant darkness, a color that made him unsuitable for long treks in the desert. Unlike Namart, Hebny sensed his delicacy and carefully picked his way without complaint among the stones, longing only to eat. When Hannu heard the cries of Namart he turned to see the horse rear above his son then lose his footing and tumble sideways. Namart's huge head hit Paneb who was knocked away as the rocks shuddered under the weight of the horse. Hannu tossed the reins to an unsure Saul who carefully led the horse across the stones.

Paneb and Namart both lay still, the boy in silence while the horse moaned. Hannu quickly cradled his son's head, holding the sleeve of his robe against the blood on his son's arm where the horse bit him. Checking Paneb's head, Hannu felt no bumps or blood and could only sit in fear as people walked around him. The Hebrews knew nothing of horses and some were scared that his huge animal, that had walked so majestically among them, could be so distressed. Hannu unwrapped the linen belt beneath his robe and quickly wrapped it around the wound on his son's arm.

Talmor walked out of the crowd, staring at the downed horse and young man. "Yet another curse of Moses!" She yelled. Her dark eyes flashed; thick hair covered her shoulders. "Here is more death and more will come if we all follow. We must save ourselves."

A deep voice from behind her called out. "At least it was an Egyptian."

Hearing this, Lior ran over the stones to the side of Hannu, looking around, seeking the deep voice.

"This Egyptian heeded the call of Moses, and God." Lior said, looking around at the crowd, "He stepped into the sea when you were ready to await death. You cried and cursed while this Egyptian showed faith in God. Are you so ready to abandon him and his kin and our leader?"

"It is a bad omen, a horrible omen, an omen of our doom," Talmor called out. "Moses is nothing, he is insane. A wind opened the seas for us, a wind can help us to go back where we can live out our lives. The Egyptians will feed us and keep us from harm. This death shows us how ignorant we have been, we must turn and go back where we belong."

"We cannot go back," the deep male voice thundered, as a large man walked out of the crowd. "But we must rid ourselves of the Egyptians, they are not like us." His name was Ori and he was tall and thick, exceedingly strong and covered with scars. Such a specimen of man was he that the abuse of the Egyptian overseers was especially harsh and would always remain fresh in his mind. He had watched these Egyptians lead their horses from Goshen, parading them in front of cripples and sore footed Hebrews. And he watched the man Hannu speak with Moses and wondered to what end. His hatred now was free as he walked barefoot over the stones as if they were soft sand.

"What do you speak of?" Lior demanded, stepping toward Ori angrily. "The Lord spared this man's son, who lays hurt, when all the others of Egypt were doomed. Do not incite idiocy lest your fool's tongue be ripped from your throat."

"And who will do that, friend of our betrayer, you? I will dispatch both you and them myself." Ori stepped toward Lior with clenched fists. His thick hair hung over a leather tunic that was torn open by his huge chest. He had been forced by the Egyptian overseers to wear leather in the heat, such was their delight in his pain.

Lior held his staff aloft as he met Ori well in front of Hannu and the fallen horse. "You will dispatch nothing, nothing, do you hear me? If you want to betray The Lord and yourself do so but harm not this man or myself or anyone."

Ori stood more than a head taller than Lior and took the staff from him easily and, breaking it in two, tossed each piece over his shoulders. Pushing the smaller man away, he strode heavily toward Hannu who sat knowing nothing of this, cradling the head of his son and speaking to him softly as Oren sat at his side, terrified for his friend. Then Lior was in front of Ori again.

"You will not do this; I will not allow it. You are not his judge."

Again, Ori pushed him aside and again Lior rose and confronted him.

"Is this why God brought us here, why He sent the Egyptian horde to their deaths in the sea? Look at them, they rise now to the surface, horses and soldiers, all dead while this man lives and cradles his son. If you do not choose to follow God then go but do not exercise your violence on them or anyone assembled here. He is not the curse," Lior said, "you are the curse. Remove yourself or follow the will of God and be silent."

Ori's eyes shone wide then darkened into slits and Lior could do nothing but stand there when deep in the crowd a voice cried out.

"Yes, be silent!" A man, much smaller than Lior, ran from the crowd and stood alone. "Be silent, you are no judge, we have all suffered. Look at me!" He was very thin but when he dropped his robe his back was as packed with welts as any man there. "Do I not know your pain? Do we not all know your pain?"

"Yes, be silent, stop this!" Another man stepped from the crowd then others within the groups repeated the words.

The cries of "Yes, be silent" rang out, above them where the beach became sand again beyond the stones, then from behind and around them and Lior and Ori both looked around in wonder.

Lior spoke softly, looking up at Ori's face. "Please, we have much work to do, we will need you."

Ori turned from Lior and roared, "You will have me let these evil harbingers live to destroy us?"

Talmor stepped forward and stood next to him. Leaning back her head she called to him as from a distance. "You have no right to do this. This is not our way. Follow me back to Egypt or go with these sheep or strike out on your own but kill no one. We have one dead already, Egyptian or Hebrew, he was with us and his death is a sign."

Lior snapped his head to her. "He is not dead."

"He is dead, or he will be soon, I see this."

Ori turned and walked off as she lifted her voice to the assembly. "Follow me to safety," she said, "the path Moses leads is to suffering and starvation. We have no food, no water, we will all die in this wilderness." She looked around and saw Moses on the slope of Baal Zephon beyond the beach. "If only we had died by the Lord's hand in Egypt!" She called out to him, though Moses was looking north and seemingly paying her no attention. "There we sat around pots of meat and ate all the food we wanted, but you have brought us out into this desert to starve this entire assembly to death."

Then she walked over the stones to where the sand reached the sea and turned again to face the people.

"I will lead us as Moses tried, to true safety, back to comfort, back to the lives we were meant to lead. Come, join me, leave this insanity."

The sisters and brothers of Talmor walked to the edge of the waters as gentle waves gave up more bodies of the army of Pharaoh. Several more Hebrews followed Talmor and then more and they murmured and argued. Namart moaned louder in his pain and Hannu's heart sparked as his son's eyes opened. Standing on the shore, people called out for others to follow into the sea. Lior looked up at Moses standing motionless, saying nothing, staring north. Why does he not speak? Is he our leader or just a mouthpiece of God?

Finally, Talmor turned and walked, the hem of her robe meeting the sea. The chill shocked her ankles as she turned to the crowd. "Come, follow, the waters will recede, God will save us." She turned and walked in up to her knees. The water pulled at her legs as if God was leading her and she accepted this sign and stepped again and again, calling out as she went deeper and deeper but none followed.

"Father," Paneb said softly, "how is the horse?"

Hannu laughed in relief then shook his head. "I do not know, my son, he seems hurt." He helped his son sit, chuckling. "Again, you worry me. I have to either take better care of you or leave you to grow as you will."

Paneb looked around, noticing the small crowd at the shore growing animated. Hannu turned to look as the mother of Talmor ran to them.

"Are you deaf?" She yelled at them frantically. "Have you heard nothing? Look, my daughter walks into the sea, she will die!"

They both looked out and watched as Talmor's head, dark hair flowing with the waves, sunk beneath the surface and her blue robe floated as if empty.

"You can move in these waters; I have seen you! You must save her!"

Hannu rose and ran off immediately. Paneb also rose quickly then stopped, his head aching. He took a moment to get his bearings before striding quickly over the stones to the beach. He reached the sandy shore and dove in after his father, swimming to where the robe floated and diving to find Talmor staring beneath the waters with wide eyes and closed mouth. Her robe whipped in the surf, first enclosing her so tight her body was shrouded, then flowing off and around her so he beheld her naked and determined.

He saw his father grab her but she fought him, prying his arms off her as she opened her mouth and sucked water in her struggle to free herself. Paneb dove and grabbed her legs and lifted and she kicked until finally Hannu gripped her tightly around her arms and waist as Paneb enclosed her legs. Kicking to propel themselves they carried her to the beach where they laid her down, coughing and angry.

Her sisters and brothers surrounded her, one cradling her head as Paneb and Hannu stepped back, watched for a moment then walked up the stony beach. People stared, some shaking their heads, as they walked by. Behind them Talmor retched but found strength and sat up and spoke.

"Egyptians!" she yelled at Hannu and Paneb, "God was with me, our God, you are not God, do not try to be God. He was with me, you are cursed, Egyptians, you will lead us to death."

Paneb turned to respond but was relieved when his father, who had not recognized Talmor, put his hand on his arm and shook his head. Talmor was surrounded and Paneb could not see her anyway. He remembered how she looked when the water was whipping her robes around. Gripping her legs after seeing her made his heart race. Hannu led him back to the injured horse, then walked up the slope to his wife and daughter.

The Hebrews became busy as their animals called out, needing to be calmed. Herds of sheep threatened to plunge up the mountain and women comforted crying children. But they were safe and a calmness settled over all as they understood what happened. Moses led them to freedom, God kept his promise and now they must make a promise to Him. Fires were built and some women took out timbrels and danced and sang a song of the defeat and death of the Egyptians.

Hannu watched then told his family to stay and he walked up the trail toward Moses who stood leaning on his staff, alone. As the words of the song rose he heard them sing of God blowing His breath, stretching out His right hand and the sea swallowing His enemies.

Hannu walked up and stood with Moses then turned and looked out at the sea again. Bodies of Egyptians were now washing up on both shores, men of faith, men of their own gods, misguided though they had been.

"There is heartache in all victories," Moses said, "children of God perish and He feels that pain."

"Even His enemies?"

"They are all His children. But his Chosen People know now what He will do for them."

Daylight brightened the morning as more bodies floated ashore and some Hebrews took it on themselves to bury the dead. Hannu was glad to feel the warmth drying his robe. "Amazing people I have joined," he said. "So sad, yet full of a strange ecstasy."

"Yes, Hannu, you see it."

"I do." He turned to Moses. "So now what happens?"

Moses looked up at the sky. The pillar of light and the cloud were both gone. "I wish I knew."

About the Author

David Shaw has written stories, articles and columns for newspapers nationwide and has been everything from a writer to a woodworker to a trucking salesman. He lives in New Jersey with his wife Elizabeth and his daughter's cat Gatsby. He can be reached at davidshawauthor@gmail.com.